Mr. Spaceman

Mr. Spaceman

a novel

ROBERT
OLEN
BUTLER

Grove Press
New York

Portions of this book previously appeared in a slightly different form
in *Louisiana Literature, The Threepenny Review,* and *Literal Latte.*

Published simultaneously in Canada
Printed in the United States of America

FIRST EDITION

Library of Congress Cataloging-in-Publication Data
Butler, Robert Olen.
  Mr. Spaceman : a novel / Robert Olen Butler.
    p. cm.
  ISBN 0-8021-1660-4
    I. Title: Mister spaceman.   II. Title.
  PS3552.U8278 M7 2000
  813'.54—dc21   99-046822

Design by Laura Hammond Hough

Grove Press
841 Broadway
New York, NY 10003

00 01 02 03 10 9 8 7 6 5 4 3 2 1

For Elizabeth Dewberry

Mr. Spaceman

1 I am. The word on the face of the bus is *LUCK*. Bright bulbs of gold illuminate the letters so that even though the night is dark, this word goes before them, shining. I am far above, but I have moved over the land and the water of this place for some years now, and so I know how it is: the hum of their tires on their Tax Dollars at Work, the rice fields sliding invisibly past and smelling like Fabric-Safe Morning Rain, spots of light out toward the night horizon where others of them huddle in their bungalows or their mobile homes waiting for what these on the bus rush to seek for themselves along Interstate number Ten. The bus dashes fast in the passing lane, the windows black, showing nothing to the outside world, but I know there are souls within, yearning forth into the dark night, crossing from the Great State of Texas to the Sportsman's Paradise of Louisiana, the Pelican State, the Bayou State, the place where they Let the Good Times Roll, and down the highway is the city of Lake Charles where strobe lights as green as the most dazzling toothbrush wave about high over the lake, restlessly sweeping an empty sky. As if they are looking for me. But from these lights, everyone passing in the night knows there are vessels here that can carry them over this water and provide games to play where they might find this thing that so many seek. This is how I understand it so far.

But the central mysteries continue to dwell in darkness. I am still learning, even at this late hour, even as the moment of my arrival is established. Even now I am trying to learn what I need to know in order to do what I must. And so I turn my attention back to the bus, still twenty miles west, blowing past a great tandem tractor-trailer, quaking in the turbulence. I am far above. I wait. I have at my disposal the Wonders of Modern Technology. I can see everything. Hear everything. I am, as those on this planet who truly believe in a widely bespirited universe call me, a *spaceman.* Or, often, an *alien.* There is some very great fear in this name *alien.* So much is alien to those who live here. Even to those who can believe in something they have never seen.

In fact, I see nothing. I hear nothing. And I think it is because of the mystery of these vanishing, fragile, powerful things that plague the dwellers in this world, things that rush from them and around them and into them and through them and out again, constantly, these *words,* these particles of *language* that they each must manufacture with their brain and body and with something else in them, too, with a *soul*—this is itself a *word,* I realize—I am putting all of this forth now in *words,* I realize, and so even beginning to try to get at the mysteries I must solve here in order to do what I must, I fall deeper into the darkness—yet I have no other word for the thing I mean but *soul*—and this is something even a spaceman knows to be a mystery, even in himself, but more so in those who dwell across the vast and strange landscape of this planet, and this is something that eludes even the wonders of the technology of my home world—and this soul is something that on this planet must try to find a way to manufacture *words,* must try to speak its insubstantial self in these tiny, hastily assembled fragments of sound, these invisible things that yet always threaten to clog my wondrously advanced machines and my wondrously advanced head, too—I speak now with self-deprecating irony, because even I am not immune to fragmentation and digression when I am forced to resort to words. The atmosphere of this planet brims with words; they blow past me and I quake in the turbulence.

I crack my knuckles. It is a soothing thing I learned from a cowboy I once beamed up from Lubbock, Texas. I am a gol-durn lucky creature. I have eight fingers full of knuckles—count 'em, eight—to crack on each of my hands, and I do this, and I grow calm, and I wait. The bus just now leaves the reach of the tandem tractor-trailer's headlight beams. There are a thousand yards of empty Interstate ahead. I wait for the bus to run farther into that dark gap. I sit before a great console, a vast screen that can flare with any of the countless images we've collected since our first visits here, long ago now, nearly a hundred revolutions of this planet around its star. Images from our machines, simply watching and listening, and images from the human voices, from the words shaping the moments from inside the brains and the souls of those who have visited us from below. All of those who came to us were dashing somewhere, all of them were seeking something. These are the images that I have to understand. Quickly now, before my appointed hour. But I am still mystified.

Perhaps this bus will help. I look again. It is racing on. For a hundred of these years we have gathered images. I am not the first. But now I am alone. I am the only one of my kind on this vessel, the only one of us attending this planet now. I am deeply moved by this responsibility. Yippee I. Yippee yay. I crack my knuckles once again. He was not a real cowboy, in the sense he himself wished for. I touch my console. He was the first of these that I had ever met. I was very young and not alone then. I call him up from the memories of this ship. I put him inside me.

I am Whiplash Willie Jones. *Mr. Griffith, of course, was the hottest of shit if you figured these moving pictures would amount to anything. I never worked for Mr. Griffith, though I could've done that if I'd got the same chance that I myself would give even to a scorpion lurking in my boot some morning. I'd at least dump him out on the floor and let him*

*have a chance to go ahead and run off and be what he is. Probably still hit
him with the boot heel, though. Smash him where he stood before he could
take a step. This maybe not the best way to put what I'm trying to say.*

*Though look at me, son. I don't have the face of Mix or Holt or my
old pal Bronco Billy Anderson. I never liked white horses anyhow. What
I'd've been, dumped out of a boot there on the floor, was what I ended
up being. The guy who grabs the loot and tries to get away. The guy who'd
as soon cheat you as look at you. The guy who'd meet a decent woman
in an orange grove in Los Angeles and marry her and take her back to
Lubbock and treat her like shit and not be able to stop himself.*

*I didn't choose any of that. That was the cards I drew even before
I knew what game it was I was playing. Take the one thing I'm remem-
bered for. It was in that little movie that Ed Porter made in 1903, The
Great Train Robbery. Ten minutes long. I show up and he puts a hat on
me and a goddamn polka-dot kerchief and he glues a handlebar mustache to my face. Then he starts the camera to watching me and he says
go here, do this, do that.*

That's how it always is, ain't it?

*So I'm the leader of the gang that robs the train in the first damn
story-telling film ever, and what happens? There's fourteen scenes in this
little tale and I get killed in an ambush in scene number thirteen, shot
dead, clear for everybody to see, and then there I am in scene fourteen,
the last one, and it's just me filling up the screen. There ain't no forest or
no horses or nothing. Just blackness all around me, but I'm alive. I been
born again. It's some kind of miracle. And what do I do? I turn and face
the audience and I raise my gun and I wrinkle my brow and I shoot. I
shoot the whole lot of them. I shoot the whole goddamn world. And it's
nothing I choose for myself. The guy behind the camera, like some voice
that just comes into my head, like the goddamn voice you hear inside
you all your life long, he says do this, and I do it. And in the theaters,
women fainted and strong men wept.*

So how could I do any better by Gladys?

Quiet now, Willie. Quiet for now. The console flickers and goes dark. It would do me no good at this moment to crack my knuckles. I have an Achy Breaky Heart, and it is best to let this voice slide back into the darkness.

I straighten up sharply. I am afraid I have let my bus go too far.

But no. I see. It is all right. The bus is rushing on alone down there. The time has come. I move my hands over the dark surface before me and I make a great light and it gathers beneath my ship and then descends like a pillar of fire and it seizes this bus and the wheels rush on, spinning wildly but touching nothing now save the air, and the bus rises quickly, so quickly that any creature there below would instantly doubt its eyes. And inside, the pilgrims seeking Luck have all fallen into a deep sleep.

I rise. I step into the brushed-smooth metalloid corridor ringing with silence. I move along quickly. Gliding, my wife says, a thing that never ceases to amuse her.

Yes. I am married. Yes, to someone from this planet. In spite of the censure of many on the planet where I come from. And there is a faint clicking now. Tiny feet dashing at me from behind. This is the approach of my wife's subspecies companion, Eddie. He is a *cat.* Or, through my wife's voice, *my darling adorable cat* or *my sweet little yellow cat* or *my cute-enough-to-eat cat*—and this latter name alarms me, I must admit, though she assures me she would never actually employ this means of admiration for Eddie—and, by extension—she has spoken, at my request, directly to this point—for me either.

Eddie dashes ahead down the corridor, anxious to see our new arrivals, I think. It is hard for me to know about Eddie. I am not telepathic with any species other than my own, even primary species. And when it comes to the subspecies, it is, of course, even more difficult. Eddie's vocabulary is severely limited. Though there is nuance to his few words. I can distinguish his put-food-before-me-instantly *meow* from his I-will-now-try-to-eat-a-piece-of-your-hand-and-it-is-not-because-you-are-cute *meow*. But there are things in his head, always, that I wish to know. He feels things very strongly, even his languor, even his serene arrogance. If there were only time, I would like to listen carefully enough to him so that I could hear. I would like to listen to every cat on this planet. To every sparrow. To every fish. But there is so little time now. I find myself moving faster along the corridor, just at the thought of this. The time is near for me. They have chosen a moment for themselves down there, the turning of a millennium. And so it shall be for me. As I hurry along this corridor I fervently hope there might be from this bus some voice, some few tracks of words, that will help me understand how to do what I soon must do with this planet.

And then she is before me. My wife. My Edna Bradshaw. My darling adorable Edna. My cascade-of-unedited-words Edna. My cute-enough-to-eat Edna. I try this thought in my head now, by her example, and I must admit there is an oddly pleasurable stirring at it.

"Greetings, my wife Edna Bradshaw," I say as I approach her. And I am struck anew with a further paradox of words on this planet. In my private inner self I am able to shape these words much more fluently and expressively than when I attempt to offer them through my mouth. On my planet we still have mouths and mechanisms to make sounds, but we use them primarily in the effort to create music or direct expressions of feeling that bypass the lumpenness of rational, denoted thought. For a time I assumed that this discrepancy between what is inside me and what comes out through my uttered words was a function of my, shall I say, *alienness*. But I no longer think that. And this is one of the reasons

I am still searching desperately for answers about the inhabitants of this planet. I believe it is the same for them.

"I'm so excited," Edna says and she does a thing with her body that still bypasses my rational thoughts quite effectively. Somehow she manages to make the tightly fitted, profusely ruffled, dramatically low-cut dress that she wears hold absolutely still while she wiggles—or I might say even undulates—within it. I am a skinny male creature, quite excessively skinny, as are all of those who inhabit my planet, the female creatures even more so. Edna is not. She is often critical of herself for this, though I think she is also quite proud of her knockers. "You have never seen a set of knockers like these, I bet." This is, for me, a memorable observation from my cute-enough-to-eat Edna. She made her observation on the occasion of our first becoming lovers, when I had asked her for a date and took her far out of her galaxy and parked in a quadrant of quiet space.

Edna's hand flies out now and thumps me on the chest. I assume she is reading the images from my inner self at this moment. But of course she is not. She will, however, occasionally thump me from an excess of love. "Oh you spaceman," she will say.

But this time she is nodding again and again toward my chest where I am still smarting from this gesture of her love. I look. I am wearing a pinstripe suit which Edna says is much too big for me but which I cannot part with, having been warmly complimented on it by a fine old gentleman we took up from a late-night diner in Chicago about thirty years ago. I had put my suit on to greet him, a suit which I had inherited from a predecessor, and Herbert Jenkins was made to feel instantly at ease by it. He had once worn a zoot suit that looked very much like this one.

"This will make everybody feel right at home," Edna says, and I focus on the lapel of my suit and a square white tag is affixed there. It reads: Hi, my Name is DESI.

She now has a similar tag in her hand and is waving it over her own chest. She says, "You know, this is a problem I simply didn't anticipate. I *am* showing a good many of my assets, am I not. And my assets don't like the idea of adhesives sticking to them. I once had a bee sting right there." She places a fingertip on the steep slope where her knockers bunch together in the middle, and without a pause—my wife Edna Bradshaw seems sometimes never to draw a breath no matter how many words she speaks—without a pause, she continues, "And it got so red and full of puss—forgive me for talking like this about unpleasant matters, but it's to the point, really. Which is, I put an adhesive bandage over that bee sting, and when I come to take it off, it felt like I was taking all my skin with it. So you see I don't have a place right at the moment to put my name tag, and you have to have name tags with strangers. I want to be a good hostess, especially this being my first time, and I'm trying to figure all this out without a great deal of guidance—I don't mean to be critical, my sweet spaceman lover—but I am struggling."

She falls silent for a moment and her hand with the tag hovers before her and then, in a burst of inspiration, quickly descends past her knockers and toward the ruffled expanse below and it thumps down there and Edna cries out in satisfaction, "That should do."

I take a step back—a necessary procedure to adjust the sight lines—and there, floating on a wave of ruffles in the center of her stomach, are the words: Hi, my name is EDNA. And I bend nearer because there is more, written in a small hand: (*Mrs. Desi, your spaceman host. Nothing to worry about.*)

I am pretty fast on the uptake. Needless to say, we have no use on my planet for such tags as these. But I perceive their function and I realize that Edna's first impulse was the correct one, to put this declaration higher on the body, so that one's eyes can take in the greeting with ease. I also understand how it is impossible—given her decision to join me in my first encounter with the new arrivals and to wear her special party dress for the occasion—for her to wear this tag in the appropriate area. I also understand, from many observations of the people of this planet, that this could cause her some social awkwardness and even embarrassment. So I gently peel the tag from my lapel and reattach it to my own middle-body area.

"What's that for, honey?" she asks.

"We will tell them it is a custom of my home planet to wear our name tags in this manner."

Edna Bradshaw smiles at me for doing this, a gentle smile, with her eyes filling, as they easily do, with tears. I am now rendered, as I usually am, utterly floppy-fingered helpless when I see her tears, even tears of appreciation and thanks, which is the case in this moment. I am struck, too, at the pleasure I am taking at her careful, indeed delicate, handwriting that identifies her as "Mrs. Desi," for she is Mrs. Desi in the fullest sense, since I am Desi and she is my wife. Desi is the name she gave me at our first meeting because none of the people here, no dweller on this planet, is capable of saying my name, my true and full name.

My wife lunges forward and embraces me. I think of the bee sting on her precious knocker and I am sad at her ordeal and very happy to be pressing against her. Across her bare shoulders and back I let my sixteen fingertips deliver my heartbeat into her. Edna once likened my fingertips to the sucker pads on the feet of certain lizards on this planet, and this has caused me a curious torment ever since. I believe her comparison was meant in a purely superficial, visual way, but the very thought, even if untrue, of some gecko down there crouching in the grass this evening, smug in his tactile knowledge of Edna's flesh—this makes me unhappy in a peculiarly intense way. I have vowed, however, never to ask my wife about this possibility. She continues her embrace, but I wish to remove these unpleasant thoughts from my mind, and I do have a bus full of sleeping and soon-to-be distressed subjects waiting for me.

"We must look in on our visitors now," I say.

Edna ends her embrace and steps back and shifts about briefly in her dress once more and pats at her hairdo, though it is stiffly inert from All the Body and Holding Power She Will Ever Need, a state attainable from certain spray cans that I periodically beam up to our vessel. Since I married Edna, it is quite remarkable, the wondrous variety of seemingly commonplace things that one of the finest fruits of my planet's technology has been used to acquire. Not that I have any regrets. My own daily life, like the lives of my fellow countrymen, can be rather stark in design: brush-textured alloys and tightly focused spot lighting and great, high-ceiling shadows. For all her stuff, which she has begun to bring into my existence, I am grateful to Edna. Personally, of course, since she is my wife, but professionally, too. These things are part of what I must try to learn.

I turn now to the great door into the Reception Hall and I move my hand and it opens. Edna and I have not discussed this moment in any detail. She asked me if she could be at my side when the next visitors arrived, and I thought this was a very good idea. There is always a period of anxiety at first, and Edna, being recognizable as one of their own, would put my visitors at ease. I said yes to her and she said she would handle everything and so I am not surprised at the name tags and the party dress. In the Reception Hall, however, there are some surprises.

The bus sits, just as it should, in a great swath of light in the center of the hall, which recedes into soothing darkness in all directions. Except one. Just as my vessel's intuitive light—as natural as a cloudless morning—immediately picks up Edna and me and moves with us as we move—so, too, has a wide column of light appeared in a space to my right, about twenty paces away from the bus. I look carefully in this direction because the things being illuminated are very strange to me. There is a large hovering drape there with red roses marching around the edges—masking a table, I realize now—and on its top is a profusion of things.

"Come and see," Edna says, taking my hand and pulling me toward the table. "This is going to be a lovely time for all. I've made everything here myself, nothing store-bought, except the ingredients, of course. That's Southern Hospitality, and if you're married to me, you're married to Southern. Course you're from the South in your own place, aren't you?"

She pauses for me to verify this. She has made this inquiry before. The distinction is uncommon where I am from and so I compute the answer again and, from what I understand, latitudinally, of her question, I am able to reassure her once more. "Yes, I am from the Southern part of my own place."

"See?" my wife Edna Bradshaw says, "this is just the touch you need. Now these are cheese straws and these are sausage balls—I had to make a choice between Jimmy Dean and Tennessee Pride, but I always tend to 'Take Home a Package of Tennessee Pride.' I like that, you know, thinking you can take home something that precious in a package, though my pride'd be Alabama pride, but never mind. At the end of the day, all you really have is just pride in your sausage, is all, and Tennessee is close enough for that."

My Edna Bradshaw pauses with this thought and an unmistakable sadness comes upon her. I will ask her about this feeling at a more appropriate moment, but already she is transforming her face into a perky, welcoming thing and she moves on down the table. She says, lifting her hand toward a great round, creviced globe remarkably similar in appearance to the outer moon of my home planet, "Now this is a pecan ball. Dried beef isn't good enough for me when I make it. This baby has three pounds of real beef jerky. You remember when I had you beam up some things from that truck stop near where I used to live? A truck driver should know good jerky, it seems to me."

I work hard at understanding what Edna is explaining to me, but the best I can do is record her observations in my memory and hope that I will one day fit all of this together. Food. Hospitality. I do know these to be crucial concepts in this world, and Edna's self-assurance in these complex matters makes me happy to have her good counsel, and—I am not reluctant to speak this, for on my planet we greatly revere learning and expertise—Edna's under-standing of these concepts makes me love her even more. She moves along the table and says, "Here's the low-fat neighborhood at our little spread. Carrot curls and rosettes of radishes. We Earth-lings are fragile creatures, for all of that. You can put that down in the book you're keeping on us, or whatever it is."

"My records are increasingly full of your wisdom," I say, though she resists the clear sexual invitation of my words. Which, I realize, is an act of the very wisdom I have spoken of, given our more pressing task at hand.

"And to top it all off," she says, "we have a little indulgence for those of our guests with a sweet tooth. A tray full of Mississippi Mud."

I quickly sort through all that I've learned about eating cus-toms on this planet and I am at a loss to find a precedent for this taste in the primary species. Or even a subspecies, for that matter. Edna laughs at the apparent display of my confusion.

"Not real mud, you silly spaceman. It's just a name. These are my best brownies with melted marshmallows, melted chocolate chips, and finely chopped pecans on top. You can see how versatile the pecan is, right here. I've used it in both a dessert and a main dish." She motions back to our deeply creviced outer moon, and then gently tugs me to the end of the table and a large bowl full of a pale green fluid. It is precisely the color of the life substance flowing in my very veins, even foaming into more substantial eddies, just as in my body. Surely this is as deceptively figurative as the Mississippi mud, this bowl of my blood, but I am suddenly intensely conscious of my hands, which is where we feel fear in our bodies on my planet. My hands grow quickly hot and threaten to stiffen.

"It's Presbyterian Punch," she says. "You're not Presbyterian, are you? Of course not. Silly me. You just look a little funny, all the sudden, and I don't want to cause any offense, though the Presbyterians I know don't take offense at much of anything."

Edna's lovely, multilayered, self-dialoging effusion of words has its usual calming effect on me and I raise my hands before me, rippling the last hot spots out of them.

"I love it when you do that," Edna says of this process. Then she adds, "Which reminds me, I want to apologize that all we have for these folks is finger food."

My hands go instantly rigid. Before me I have sixteen oaken trunks in terrified uprightness waiting for a strike of lightning: I put it thus to embrace the metaphorical impulses of this planet and, as is the great benefit of our ability to take on the perspectives of those we are near, I suddenly understand one more figurative turn of speech.

Edna says, "I forgot to have you beam me up some plastic utensils."

"Of course," I say, dropping my hands out of sight. "So these visitors must use their fingers to eat the food you have prepared."

"We can do a sit-down dinner later," Edna says, and then her words veer off sharply, something I have learned to be prepared for. "Hi, honey," she cries. "Welcome. It's all right."

I am determined to keep up with her. "Hi, honey," I reply in a similarly excited voice. "Certainly a sit-down dinner will be all right." But I realize that her gaze is no longer directed at me. She is looking over my shoulder, and I turn to see what it is.

The bus waits in the light. The windows are dark-tinted but near the front is a face pressed hard against the glass, gaping, eyes wide in terror, taking in all of this. The face presses harder, the eyes widen even further, and I understand that I am myself the source for this surge of distress. My face is different in many respects from the faces on this planet. My wife Edna Bradshaw has always spoken lovingly of my quite large eyes that resemble in shape Eddie the cat's eyes and my total lack of hair or fur of any kind and my mouth that is thin and sinuous—I have a very nice mouth by my home planet's standards, but it has nothing like the outfold of lips that I must say I find enchanting in Edna. I understand how the sudden turning of this man in the large suit—that is, me—and his having a face like mine would cause the fear I see in the bus window. It is hard to look directly upon me. All of our visitors over the years have had to come to terms with our faces, one way or another. But in these first moments I am usually wearing my wide-brimmed felt hat to soften the effect.

The face vanishes from the window and Edna brisks past me. "Come on, Desi. These folks need some food."

2 And so it has come to pass that the twelve sojourners on the bus that carries *LUCK* upon its face have disembarked into the Reception Hall of my vessel and have each been given a name tag by my wife Edna Bradshaw, though she struggled at times, her Magic Marker in hand, to make them understand what she wished from them, for they were groggy from the deep sleep induced by our acquisition beam, and names are fragile things, after all. And these visitors are groggy still, though one of them has just now approached the delicious and welcoming food prepared by my wife. This is a good sign, even though most of them continue to drift uncertainly about the hall.

Normally in this process, before Edna Bradshaw was my wife, I would take these visitors straight from the bus to the warm and comforting darkness of the rooms prepared for them on our vessel. Then I would soon begin to interview them, bringing forth their voices and listening to and recording them in the vast and sparkling energy fields of our memory machines from where we can draw these voices back, again and again, and become one with them. This is our process. But tonight I am content to let the good times roll. This group has been specially chosen. These twelve are destined to help me in this time of my greatest challenge. It will soon be a very great challenge for their whole planet, as well. And so, for tonight, I stand beside the table of food. They drift to me—are herded to me, actually, by the charm and energy of my wife Edna Bradshaw—and I say, "Have a cheese straw. Have a sausage ball. Have a cup of cold Presbyterian Punch to quench your thirst."

15

I have been saying things like this for many minutes and I have been met only with glazed stares or startled leaps. I have just begun to fear that I have made a mistake; they should be in their dark spaces, sleeping, resting, adjusting. But a few moments ago, a young man perhaps twenty-three or twenty-four years old stopped before the table and looked at the food and he shook his head violently and he pressed the heels of his hands into his eyes and then he dropped his hands and opened his eyes again, wide, trying to come to terms with what was before him.

His tag says, Hi, my name is JARED. So I say, "Please, Mr. Jared, take that silver knife and cut a chunk off the outer moon of my home planet." This is a little joke, based on my previous thoughts about the pecan ball, though I instantly realize that he has no frame of reference to allow him to see the humor.

My dear Edna appears at his elbow. "Go on ahead. It's a real pecan ball. I don't understand that moon stuff either." She gives me a wink, to let me know that her implicit criticism of me is itself a little joke, and then she begins to cut the pecan ball for this young man. She continues, "My husband thinks everybody would just automatically know about his home planet. Like my daddy'd sometimes say something he clearly expected me to understand about Mobile and I didn't have a clue. See, I'm from Bovary, Alabama, and that's a far thing from Mobile, let me tell you, and I'm not talking about miles. I only went to Mobile once and I didn't like it, though I've been some places even farther than that with my husband the spaceman and I liked them a lot. That's him there, Jared, looking at you with those big old eyes. He's a good man, I can tell you. A sweet and kind man and so you can just eat your pecan ball with a peaceful mind."

Jared blinks at me and looks at the chunk of pecan ball on the paper plate in his hand and then he makes a tiny snapping movement with his head—I have seen this gesture many times over the years—and I know he is fully present at last. This has always been a difficult moment for visitors, the first understanding that this is not a dream, but Jared surprises me. He lifts his paper plate slightly toward Edna and speaks as if we have long been engaged in a casual conversation. "So'd you make this yourself?"

"What a sweet boy," my wife says. "Yes, I did."

"Cool," Jared says to Edna. "You're human, right? From Earth?"

"From Alabama."

"Where'd you two meet?"

Edna is already cutting another piece of the pecan ball for Jared, though he has not yet begun to eat what he has. She says, "In the parking lot of the all-night Wal-Mart Supercenter in Bovary. He'd been listening to me with his machines." She deposits more of the pecan ball on the young man's plate.

"We can hear all your words," I try to explain, "but through the machines they are very confusing. And so, What is a Guy to Do? That is why we need to be Oh So Much Closer and then we can Get to Know You Better."

And from across the Reception Hall a woman's voice cries out "Oh my god!"

"Oh dear," Edna says.

With a look of suddenly remembering a thing forgotten, Jared says, "Where's Citrus?"

"Arthur!" the woman's voice cries.

"There's lime sherbert in the punch," Edna says.

"My girlfriend," Jared says. He looks around, "There she is."

I follow his gaze even as the woman's voice calls out "Arthur!" once more and Edna excuses herself and moves off.

Away from the others, standing with her face turned up, faintly smiling into the dark, her body clothed such that it is nearly indistinguishable from the shadows, is a young woman with a spiky spray of deep-space black hair and black lips and a dozen tiny glints of metal about her face—rings and studs that she has attached to her flesh as if her very image would fly apart without these connecting devices.

A body lurches near, cutting off the girl in black. I read, Hi, my name is TREY. This man, clearly still not fully present, mumbles, "Slots. Where are the goddamn slots. Seen the goddamn buffet four times already, but no slots." And he is gone.

"Citrus, hey," Jared calls, his mouth full of pecan log, bits of the nuts spewing mistily into the spot lighting around us. The young woman continues to smile toward the invisible ceiling.

"She is not quite awake," I say.

Jared looks at me. He, too, has metal on his face, though only a bit, two rings in an ear. He waves what is left of his pecan ball in a vague, sweeping gesture, meaning, I believe, to draw my attention to the entire spaceship. He says, "I knew there was something like this going on in the universe. You know? It's, like, the thing I really expected."

"You are a prescient young man," I say.

Edna arrives now with her arm intertwined with the arm of a small, elderly woman, VIOLA, according to her name tag. "This is my husband, Desi," Edna says.

"Citrus!" Jared calls.

Viola is frozen, wide-eyed, gazing at me, and Edna looks toward Jared's girlfriend, whose face has descended now, though is still uncomprehending. "Oh," Edna says, "you mean Judith?"

Jared barks in laughter. "Judith? She's not Judith anymore. She's long past Judith."

"Well, honey, that's the name she gave me for her tag," Edna says, and she turns her attention back to the woman on her arm.

"Come on now, Viola, his eyes are real pretty, don't you think?" She is referring to my eyes, trying to deal with Viola's astonishment at the sight of me.

"Did she really tell you 'Judith' was her name, Mrs. Desi?"

"You're such a sweet boy."

"Arthur!" Viola cries, though in a less strident voice, a fully conscious voice.

"Her name is Citrus." Jared, who seemed so quickly at ease with his new surroundings, now sounds Dried Up, Tied and Dead to the World. He looks sadly down at his plate of pecan log.

A man's angular face, dark from an African heritage, appears, floating behind Edna's head with only blackness all around. His eyes fix on me and he brings forth a rich, mellifluous, and ringingly loud voice: "Your honor, why in the motherfuck is the jury out of its box? What's all this milling about?"

"Whoa," Jared says. "What's his problem?"

Now the face floats to the side and a whole man emerges into the spot of light, which glares off his name tag: Hi, my name is HUDSON. He wears a dark suit tailored tightly to cling to him in the way I think Edna wishes for my suit to fit.

I try to relieve Jared's mind. "Did you hear how this clearly educated man expressed himself, Mr. Jared? You are all emerging slowly from a state of suspension. You will all speak for a while using words from the unswept refuse of your minds. Your Citrus no doubt called herself Judith in that state."

"If the jury won't sit, then they must acquit!" Hudson cries.

"You see? He quotes perhaps from a poet he has long forgotten."

"Arthur! Help!" Viola is looking desperately around.

"Come on, honey," Edna says to her. "Let's go find him." The two women move off and Hudson draws nearer, squinting at my face.

"What kind of judge are you?" he says. "A Reagan appointee?"

I motion to my name tag and Hudson focuses instead on my hand, squinting harder.

Jared tries to explain. "He's a spaceman. An alien. This is the start of the new millennium, see. We're on his spaceship and we're heading into some other galaxy to be studied as representatives of Earth, since all these older generations of ours have fucked up our planet so bad and these superior beings are scared to death of us. Right?"

I say, "You are in touch only with partial truths in this matter, Mr. Jared, though I appreciate your efforts to be of assistance."

"I'm having trouble focusing my eyes," Hudson says.

"Hi, my name is Desi." I read this for him with what I hope is a bright and cheery voice, following the example of my wife, as the man named Trey drifts past again pumping his hand oddly in the air before him and saying a word over and over that I have not heard: "Ka-ching."

Hudson draws up to full height, taller than me by a full head.

"Would you like some sausage balls?" I ask him. "They are Tennessee Pride." But I realize he is about to snap fully awake.

"Citrus! Over here!" Jared lifts his plate of pecan ball as if to entice her and Hudson looks at the young man, trying hard to think clearly. Jared sighs loudly and puts his plate down and moves off toward his girlfriend. And two more visitors appear at the far end of the table, side by side, a young man and a young woman, perhaps a little older than Jared, showing an Asian heritage in their faces.

The young man says, "Have I forgotten that it's Tet?"

"I don't think so," says the young woman. "This is food I don't recognize."

They both bend near the cheese straws, studying them carefully.

"What the fuck is this?" Hudson has begun a slow revolution and I can hear in his voice a fully restored clarity of mind. I missed the moment of his snap, and he clearly missed an initial glimpse of his host Desi the Spaceman. His back is to me. I reach to pull my stylish wide-brimmed black felt hat lower over my face, but it is not on my head. I am, instead, dressed for my wife Edna Bradshaw's welcome party.

"I should have rented a goddamn car," Hudson says aloud, though clearly addressing only himself, and he is coming back around, looking at the young Asian couple, who are motionless before the sausage balls, and then at the full spread of the table, and now his eyes fall on me and he draws back. Suddenly he is wading through deep and muddy waters.

"Hi," I say. "My name is Desi. I am a friendly guy."

"A friendly guy? A fucking friendly guy? You got nothing to do with 'guys' from what I can see." Hudson suddenly staggers a little at the import of this. "Oh man."

"I understand your concern, Mr. Hudson," I say.

"You look like . . . I'm not going to say it. I will not say it. Is this an abduction? Is that what this is?"

"You are on a spacecraft," I say. "But not to worry."

"Of all the goddamn times, Wilhelmina. Of all the mother-fucking times for you to pack your bag and grab the Lexus. And I *had* to go off and shoot some craps, didn't I. Like it'd turn my luck around. Even if it meant riding the fucking bus." Hudson has first addressed a person named "Wilhelmina" and then has begun speaking to himself, though he is still in my presence and is mostly looking at me. I attribute this phenomenon—which I have observed often in years of interviews—to the properties of spoken words. The words yearn to reach out directly to this or that soul but in the process of coming into being, they take on the finite proper-

ties that make them what they are, a limitation they themselves recognize and then try to ignore by conjuring up the ears of others who
cannot hear or inner parts of the self that are oblivious to reason.

And at this moment Edna arrives. Viola is still on her arm.
On her other arm is an elderly man, ARTHUR, with a great, up-
standing shock of white hair and his outer arm is thrown around
the shoulder of a stocky man with a footprint of shining baldness
but long gray sideburns and a ponytail, and this is HANK, who
has his own arm thrown around Arthur, and Edna says, "Viola and
I have found Arthur, and he'd already found Hank. Hank's the
driver of the bus, but he also happens to be Arthur's brother from
a past life. Isn't that a coincidence, Desi?"

Viola says, "What's happening to us?"

"Your husband and Mr. Hank have not quite yet come to their
senses," I explain. "This impression of theirs will pass."

"We're brothers," Arthur says.

"I'm younger in this life, but I was the older brother before,"
Hank says, squeezing hard at Arthur's shoulder and shaking him
so that I hear a rattling sound from his mouth.

"I don't remember that," Arthur says.

"Trust me, little buddy," Hank says.

"Are you people crazy?" Hudson suddenly cries. "What are
you talking about? We've all been kidnapped onto a fucking
spaceship."

"Please, Mr. Hudson," Edna says, though very sweetly. "You
shouldn't use those words. There are ladies present."

Hudson violently shakes his head, trying to snap himself
once more. But there are no more snaps available to him. This is
real. He looks at Edna and then at Viola and then at me and he
forces his voice into a carefully modulated tone. "You're right.
Though not because of the ladies. I have the full rich range of

the English language at my command. I am a graduate of Harvard Law. No matter what the stress, I do not need to go back to the fucking streets." He stops and growls at the sudden reappearance of this word, even in the midst of his declaration of independence from it.

I have no power of telepathy with this man, but he is a well-educated man, a self-aware man, and I feel certain he is contemplating the odd way that the words of his planet can seem to take on a kind of sentience, a *will*. The *words* are the independent entities in this place, not the speaker. Though this is not true of me. I am not a natural breeding place for words. I am unable even to express these very thoughts to Hudson in this moment, though I am sure if I could he would be put at ease, a bond would be forged between us like the bond between Hank and Arthur, a bond, by the way, that is even now dissolving, for Hank seems to have snapped and is examining his arm around this narrow-shouldered, white-haired stranger beside him.

"What the fuck?" Hank says.

Hudson snorts a short, ironic laugh, though it is a further mystery of the *words* of this world that Hank's form of *fuck* has a soft, almost affectionate edge to it, quite different in mood from Hudson's.

Hank withdraws his arm and then he looks at me and he recoils.

And a great and ravenous crunching begins down the table and then a loud cry of "I *adore* carrots!" I look and there is a supplementary "I adore them!" and both declarations are remarkably clear, given the bulge of carrots in the cheeks of the speaker, a slender woman with eyes quite attractively large for her species and knockers to rival even Edna's. She stuffs more carrot curls into her mouth with both hands. Her name is MISTY.

Just beyond her, the couple with Asian heritage have turned and are riveted by the sight of Misty's mouth, the carrots crowding in, the churning of the puffed cheeks. I see their name tags now. She is MARY. And he carries, overtly, a form of this group's governing word on his own chest: LUCKY.

"Yo. Desi." This is Hudson's voice. "Listen up."

A man has just arrived behind Misty. He puts his arms around her and instantly cups her breasts in his hands. She does not respond to this at all, except to address him. "Digger baby. Carrots."

"Misty wisty," Digger says in a tiny child's voice, though he is a big man, as tall as Hudson. He has a heritage from a Caucasian race but his skin is quite dark. I recognize this as the effect of prolonged exposure to this planet's star. He says, "Want to play in the dark with your wildcatter's big old Rotary Drill?"

Misty can stuff no more carrots into her mouth. She lowers her face a little and tries to chew, seeming not even to consider Digger's dream-state proposition.

"Desi," Hudson says.

My attention is still caught by Digger's hands—he is even DIGGER on his name tag. His hands squeeze now at Misty's Full Figured Pride and Joy. Clearly she recognized those hands instantly, for she did not look over her shoulder to identify him. I think about my wife Edna Bradshaw, whether she would know her husband Desi from simply the touch of my hands on her knockers.

"*Mister* Spaceman," Hudson says.

I turn to Hudson now and I observe, "Of course she would. There are eight fingers on each hand."

"Say what?"

This makes me stop. My observation was not intended for Hudson. "How interesting," I say. "Perhaps words with their own wills do breed now within me." I stop again. "Even that was not intended for you. Or that. Or that. Or that."

I cease all my words, breathless with discovery.

"I demand to know what you have in mind for us," Hudson says.

And a gunshot rings out.

"Jesus," Hudson cries and Viola screams and I reach toward Edna to pull her to me, to shield her, and I will shield Viola, too, recognizing the sound from my years of study of this planet, and Hudson is grabbing at Hank and Arthur, who are nearest to him, and he says, pressing them toward the floor, "Down. Quick." And my hands are on Edna's shoulders and she is quiet, turning her head to look toward the sound, and I pull at her and Viola trails with her, but now, as Arthur and Hank sink down with Hudson, I can see across the Reception Hall, and before the bus stands a woman with her arm straight up, and the pistol, still smoking, is in her hand, pointing toward the ceiling. She has a puzzled look on her face.

I let go of Edna and I slip past her and glide quickly across the space. We can move very speedily when we wish, we who are the primary species from my planet, though I do not want to alarm this woman. I near her and she is compact, with a sharply tailored woman's suit in Power Red for the Career Woman on the Go, and I calculate that if she panics from my very rapid approach and the look of me, then only I would be in peril from the next discharge of the weapon, and I find that preferable to further unaimed panic shots. I also need quickly to make a single, clear public statement to all these visitors, for I strongly suspect that this sudden noise has instantly snapped the rest of them out of their befuddled states.

And I am before her and she has lowered the pistol and is pointing it at the center of my chest, though she does not seem clearly to understand that she is doing this. Her eyes are wide upon my face. This is not unexpected. Her hand is unsteady. Her purse is open and lying at her feet. "Well then," I say. "I see by your name tag that you are CLAUDIA."

Technically, she is clearheaded now, but there is too much for her to take in, all of a sudden. "Your name tag," I repeat, feeling this would be a comforting thing for her to observe. She does look down at the tag on her lapel. As she does, my hand goes out and enfolds hers.

"I suspect you do not even know you are holding this," I say and I gently disengage the pistol from her hand, and she yields the thing readily.

"Where am I?" she asks. "What are you?"

"These are relevant questions," I say. "Your fellow visitors are seeking the same answers."

And I turn now and I suddenly understand a figure of speech I have always found distasteful. All eyes are on me. I could never overcome my impulse to visualize that literally. But now I understand. I feel these eyes as separate, palpable points of pressure. These eyes, most of them wide with fear, are *on* me, and I am a nervous wreck. In this moment I find the always elusive words of this planet even more difficult to shape in my mouth.

"Hi," I say. "My name is Desi. I am a friendly guy. There is a Kind of Hush All Over the World Tonight. I Would Like to Teach the World to Sing. I Would Like to Buy the World a Coke."

"But tonight we only have Presbyterian Punch," Edna says. All eyes are now on her. I am glad. I have many complex things to explain, but I am hearing my words as if I were hovering in my space vessel high above them and I were hearing them from below, through our machines. Edna is continuing. "For those of you who don't know, that's lime sherbert and ginger ale. But Desi can get you some Cokes if any of y'all prefer."

Edna pauses, probably only for a breath, and I appreciate her efforts to make up for my inarticulateness, but this is my responsibility, and I say, "This is my wife Edna Bradshaw." She waves to everyone and their eyes return to me. "We are a happy couple. Only Her Hairdresser Knows for Sure."

Edna laughs. "Oh Desi, you spaceman." Then she addresses our visitors. "I *was* a hairdresser when we met. He's such a kidder."

"Your Love Has Put Me at the Top of the World," I say to Edna, and I realize that it is from a true feeling that has just come over me.

But the man named Digger cries, "What do you want from us?"

This is not where my head is at. I realize that Digger's question is on the minds of all the others, more than the topic of my relationship with Edna Bradshaw, though I think the fact of my marriage should offer some reassurance to them. I focus on the question of Mr. Digger. I say, "I want only to speak with you. I want you to be my guests for a brief time and you can tell me about your life on this planet."

Now Viola's voice quavers up, though I cannot see her. "Are you going to hurt us?"

Edna says, "Desi wouldn't hurt a fly. He's the sweetest, gentlest man—well, as he'd put it, male of a primary species—in the whole universe."

There is a long moment of silence. Then Hudson calls out, "What if we don't want any part of this?"

"You do not have to speak with me," I say.

"What if we want to go back to Earth right now?" he says.

This is a touchy point, since I have brought a diverse group of visitors here all at once. I struggle to find the right words. They must go back as a group, but I do not wish for any of them to feel incarcerated.

Edna once again steps in. She says, "I understand y'all were going to the casinos in Lake Charles to gamble. Well, my Desi happens to be the smartest man I've ever known. If you just stay and visit with us for a little while, I bet he can teach you how to win big. Y'all have found your luck in him."

A murmur ripples through the hall at this. I can feel each of my visitors' quest for *LUCK* come upon me, like their eyes, as points of insistent pressure on my body. I do not know if I can do what Edna says, but I feel a surge of belief in the room, a belief that is burrowing now into me in a dozen places. After all the years of my work on this planet, this is a new thing.

"Is that true? Can you teach us?" This is the voice of the man named Trey.

And I answer, "Do not be afraid. Follow me, pardners."

3 There are certain powers that I have. One is to make these creatures sleep. My vessel is large and has many rooms. Each of my guests is dreaming now in a sweetly shadowed space. I have placed Claudia's pistol in the Hall of Objects. It is late and I am very weary. But I sit before my console surrounded by darkness. I would sing now for myself, using my voice for its true purpose, but unspoken words from this planet cling to the roof of my mouth, my tongue, the inner surfaces of my cheeks, and they block the way. I hum instead. Another of the powers that I possess is the power to listen. To set a visitor from this planet speaking and to provide the delicate balance of light and shadow and ozone and hum of silence and nibble of sleep so that the visitor will open and find a voice to tell of the welter of things inside, to tell of the things that I intently hope will add up to the essence of the creatures of this place. And though I have no telepathy with my visitors, after they have spoken, I have the power to recall their voices and bring them inside me, to become the speakers. And I do this so that I might listen for the hidden music—a very difficult task, since the instrument of these voices is plucked only on the thin strings of *words*—but I listen very closely to the voices, straining to hear in them the song of the ethos, so that I may know.

For I must know. To do what I have been given to do, I must know. My hand goes to the console, to play the directive once more. But I have wearied of that. It no longer lifts me up. I wish the cup to pass from me. Let some other spaceman drink of this place. I lift my hands to crack my knuckles. But they prove to be uncrackable, for I have gone all stiff-fingered. I am not just weary at the thought of this thing I must do, I am afraid. On the eve of this planet's new millennium, on the division of light and dark that they call the thirty-first of December, at the end of the revolution of their planet around their star that they have reckoned to be the two thousandth from the birth of a mysterious and influential figure in their history, on that evening, which fast approaches, I have been charged to find an appropriately public place and to make my vessel visible and then to descend from it in my true self and thus reveal to all the inhabitants of this planet this great and fundamental truth of the cosmos.

The console is dark. I wish to close my eyes. But I am humming my way into a reprise. Ah, reprise: the familiar thread of music taken up once again. Double Your Pleasure, Double Your Fun. Set 'em up again, Barkeep. These are the Times of Your Life. I am in a nostalgic mood. Already words are piling up in me. But instead of my own imperfect, word-bedraggled voice, it is a voice that exists beyond me that I seek. Perhaps it is the influence of Whiplash Willie Jones, but I am drawn once more back to my early days hovering over this planet, late in the sixth decade of this century. There was a woman who visited from a dark hilltop in the state of Virginia. I spoke with her in the time of deep shadows on our vessel. The two others of my species were sleeping. But I was awake. I was very young. And Minnie was awake. She was very old, by the standards of the primary species of this planet. She had arrived that morning and she had no fear of us, from the first moments. I found her in the corridor. She was standing still, her eyes closed, her head tilted slightly. I asked her what she was doing. She said that she was listening for the engines of our craft.

I think of her and I know she has gone from this life and I draw a quivering breath and my fingers wave before me, slowly, as if they are under water, like an anemone. I pass one of these grieving hands over the console and her voice comes forth and I put her inside me.

I am Minnie Butterworth. *Papa would let me go off some days, just to walk and think and dream. He knew I took things hard. He wanted me to marry, but I was trying to feel right inside myself first. Still, why should he have paid me any mind? That wasn't an era when you'd indulge a girl-child like that. Still isn't, but it was even worse then. Papa was a good man. Mama was dead, but my older sister, Maidie, took care of most of the daily things. She and her husband, John, lived with us. John was a fisherman with Papa and they worked Kitty Hawk Bay and Albemarle Sound, staying away from the big boats out on the ocean. They were strong men and they had courage, but they weren't fools. The Atlantic up and down the Outer Banks was a widowmaker. They didn't want to die.*

Maybe I got a little of Papa's caution. Maybe that was the difference in how my life went. I don't know. But there's only so much you can do to control your fate. Look at Mama. She never went near the boats and she ended up drowning. That was in the great hurricane of 1899. I was eighteen and she was barely twice that. I can see now how young she was, looking back. The water came in and we went up in the attic and Mama looked down and her Singer sewing machine was just disappearing under the water and something took her. She only said a few words, like 'My Singer,' and she went on down, I guess to try to drag it up the stairs. Though of course that was impossible. It was a big thing bolted to its own table with wrought-iron legs. Papa was over in the other side of the attic and by the time he came across and down the stairs to follow her, she'd disappeared.

After that, Maidie got married and I'd help around the house. I'd go out with the women of Kitty Hawk and we'd make and mend the nets. I'd tend our garden. Some young men of the town courted me. But some-

thing wasn't right. I'd go out when I could on my own, to walk. The dunes above Kitty Hawk Bay had growths of all kinds of trees, trying to make a go of it. Cedar and oak and sassafras and locust and sycamore and persimmon. And in the damp places between the dunes there were gums and cypresses and some old, fat-trunked pines. But there was such wind. All the time. The sands would roll in and blow the trees down and cover them over in big, crescent dunes. Whaleheads, we'd call them.

The day I'm thinking of was in December of 1903. I was in a bad mood. Some young man or other was pressing me to get serious. Papa was pressing me to listen to the young man. I just walked off that morning. It was the middle of the week and the wind was fierce, coming in from the north. For the better part of the year the wind blew from a little west of south, but in the winter it came straight down from the north pole, which nobody'd ever been to, at that time. I could've gone off and just hid in the trees, like I usually did. But sometimes you feel like going ahead and making things worse. A little bit of homeopathy. And if it didn't work like that as a cure, then at least you could wallow in things and feel sorry for yourself.

So I struck off to the south, toward the Kill Devil Hills. Things down there would be about as gloomy as I could make them. I even passed a place where the winds had laid bare a cemetery. There were bones of dead people scattered all about, as cheap and naked as fish bones. I don't know if that made me think of my mother. I can't remember now, all these years later. It should have. And if it did, maybe I was reminded how your life wasn't really your own. Which would be an answer of sorts to the question that has always blown around and around in my head: Why did my life go on as it did?

Anyway, I kept walking, and after about four miles, I got tired and I lay down in some beach heather on the westward slope of a little hill. I'd come up to it from the Albemarle side and I could hear the ocean crashing in the distance, though I hadn't seen it yet. It seemed very far away from where I lay, and I may have dozed for a little while.

And then I awoke to a remarkable sound. I sat up straight and quick. It was a metallic rumble, full of pops and sputters. I knew it was an engine of some sort. I'd been to the mainland the year before and seen a couple of the new motorcars, which I loved. But this sound was coming from over the peak of the hill and I figured it wouldn't be there for long. I scrambled to the top and I stood up, and there it was. At first I didn't understand what it would do. It was laid out on a long track and for a moment I thought it must be a strange sort of railroad engine.

But it had wings. Sweet Jesus in heaven, it had wings. I could not name the parts at the time or recognize the things of the earth that they were made of, but I was taking them in like the features of the face of the man you'd just fallen in love with at first sight: the two great braced main wings, the twin horizontal elevators in front, the twin vertical rudders behind, all made of ash and spruce and muslin, and those engines, also at the rear, crying out to me, the two pusher propellers spinning into invisibility. And at that precise moment no human being had yet ever made a powered flight into the air and I saw the man lying prone in the center of the great lower wing and instantly I wished to be there in his place. Already, I wanted this act for myself. I stood there with the wind pounding at me, the same wind that was even then gathering beneath these wings, ready to lift them, I stood there and my dress was billowing and whipping around my legs and my hair had come undone and was unfurled from my head like a wind sock and I watched this wonderful thing that I loved instantly as it moved along its track gathering speed and my heart beat wildly and then this thing made of trees and cloth lifted up. It flew.

There would come an age, not too many years later, when there would be women who flew airplanes. I had the heart of any of them. I had the yearning. But I left the Kill Devil Hills that afternoon in Decem-

ber in 1903 with a desperate desire and no hope of ever fulfilling it. None. I was who I was. I cried out to myself some few words of this desire and I went down the steps and into the water and I was overwhelmed. I married the next year. I made a home for my husband who chose not to fish but to become a lumberman instead and he took us to Virginia and gave me three fine babies who became three fine sons who went off to do what they wished with their lives. But in the dark nights, with my husband sleeping beside me and the wind blowing the trees outside, I was unfaithful to him, again and again. I lay down with a great wing and there was the sound of its engine inside me and its propellers pressed me forward and into the sky.

Minnie's voice disappears now from inside me. It flies off into one of those dark nights of hers, fifty years ago or more. But still remaining is the first night that Minnie Butterworth was on a spaceship and I found her awake and wandering our corridors. I arranged for her to speak to me then. I made the wind to blow for her and made her feel lifted up, and these words flowed out of her mouth and into me like a Big Gulp, like a Mondo Thirst Quencher.

But I knew that Minnie thirsted still.

So I said to her, "You are on a spaceship now."

"I figured," she said. "I was listening for your engines, but I couldn't hear them."

"They make no audible sound," I said. "We are near to your home, though many miles above. Would you like to take us somewhere else?"

I could hear Minnie's breath catch in her chest. But she narrowed her eyes at me, a gesture that even in that early stage of my research I understood to betoken suspicion.

I stood and took her by the arm, very gently, and I walked her from the interview room, down the corridor, and into the command center. I placed her in the first commander chair and I sat in the second. Even the nearly obsolete model of our basic vessel that we flew in mid-century could easily have been commanded by one, but, fortunately, there were still two places, mostly for wormhole navigation.

I moved my hand over the panels and the great screen before Minnie Butterworth flashed into a vast image of her home planet as seen from our ventral eye. It was at this moment that Minnie let herself understand and believe what it was that I offered. Instantly her eyes filled with tears.

I make a connection now, late in my present night, alone before my New and Improved panels. I have always felt a tender thing for the quickness of the tears of my wife Edna Bradshaw. I realize that this trait in her has inevitably stirred—in the deep, singing part of me, the wordless true part of me—a memory of Minnie Butterworth on the night that she flew.

Minnie said to me in a faint voice, "Is it possible?"

I replied, "The World is Your Oyster. This is the New Thrill in Travel Planning." And I passed my hand over the navigation panel before Minnie and it came alive. I lifted her hand and laid it palm-to-palm against mine. Her breath caught again, and I folded my eight fingers around her and let her take in the beat of my heart, to reassure her. I said, "You need only move your hand above this light."

And she took her hand and she moved it and she saw her planet slide easily under her and she laughed and she wept and she flew. She flew around her planet many times that night and out into the darkness, out past her moon and around and back again. Minnie Butterworth flew farther and faster than anyone had ever flown in the history of her species and I sit now quaking in the dark at the thought of her and I feel that I am close to understanding something. Close. But farther away at the same moment. And the voice of Edna Bradshaw is near me.

"Darling spaceman," she says. "Come to bed."

4 I still cannot sleep. So Edna forgoes sleep herself. She sits reading beside me in the bed, radiant in her Antique-Pink Bare-Essential Babydoll with the Eye-Catching Uplift of Underwire Cups and the Adorable Enticement of Cleavage Ribbon Ties. Her book has a woman showing much the same great swath of her chest, as she is bent back by a man with a three-corner hat and a black eye-patch. Our bed is Awash with Swashbuckling Passion, but the suckers on the tips of my fingers are clamped tight from my sleeplessness.

Edna Bradshaw is a very good wife. Her eyelids droop from her own weariness but she has turned aside my sincere urgings to retire ahead of me. It would take only a wave of my hand—there is energy field enough in it, even this late—to encourage a roll of words from Edna. I feel a little guilty, having heard Minnie Butterworth tonight, not to become part of Edna's voice, at least briefly. Of course, I never felt for Minnie the way I do for Edna Bradshaw, not as a husband for a wife. But still, the voice is an intimate thing. Such an intimate thing, really. And I did secretly break one of our prime operational directives for Minnie Butterworth. I let her keep her memory of us when I returned her to the surface of her planet. She promised to hold our secret close and I knew I could trust her and I wanted her always to know what she had done. She came to me as she was about to go and she gave me a kiss on the cheek—the first such, I believe, that any of us had ever received from this species.

Ah. Listen to me. I say "species" and this word that rationally and precisely denotes the concept to which I was referring suddenly sounds, in my deepest part, stridently out of tune. I become, with simply the use of that *word,* a creature of ghastly aloofness, a Monster from Outer Space. My hands go up and grind at my face now.

"What is it, Desi?" Edna's voice sings softly into my mind.

I do love this woman.

And it happens again. As soon as I categorize Edna Bradshaw with *that* word, I have a terrible feeling inside me. Yes, she is, of course, a *woman.* I do love *this woman.* But to use the word sucks the warmth out of her, stacks her, naked and pink and wrapped Freezer Fresh Every Time on a shelf, with all the other *women* of this world.

I say, "Would you know my hands if I came up from behind and put them on your knockers?"

"Of course," she says. "You've got eight fingers on each hand."

"No," I say. "I ask something more than that. If I had only five fingers on each hand. Would you know me by my touch? If I came up and put my hands on you and squeezed?"

"I'm sure I would, Desi honey. I know every little thing about you."

I am happy beyond reason for that, though I realize there are still unanswered questions regarding this process. But I have gone quite floppy-fingered.

I am Edna Bradshaw's husband, officially, by the customs of my home planet, and I am Edna Bradshaw's Spaceman Lover, by the customs of her former colleagues at Mary Lou's Southern Belle Beauty Nook in Bovary, Alabama. My hands are ready to initiate the actions that are most commonly associated with intimacy on this planet, given either role. But my cute-enough-to-eat Edna seems very tired and I choose instead to place her nearer to her dreams and, as intimacy is understood on my planet, even closer to me. Though on my planet we do not use the prophylactic of words with our voices. Be Safe, Be Sorry. I wave my hand and she sighs and drifts and I bring forth her voice to put inside me. I suggest a direction, gently, though this is not always effective: "Tell me about the sadness you feel at the pride in your sausage."

Edna looks about and then finds my eyes and the sounds begin, my own mouth moving in synchronicity. *The party went so well, don't you think? At least until the gun went off. It's not easy to cook for strangers, especially when they could be from all sorts of places other than Alabama. Sausage. Oh my. So much depends on sausage. You take a one-pound roll of sausage and there are so many things to consider. Spicy or mild, for instance, though if there's strangers with foreign tastes, you should always err on the conservative side. You choose the mild sausage, and if you're making it into sausage balls, Kraft American cheese. If they want a sharp cheese, then you can let them find that somewhere else along the table, if it's big enough, or for their next meal. If all they've got is what you're giving them and all you can give them is one thing, then better safe than sorry when it comes to spice.*

You need a good biscuit mix, and that's a choice right there, though I'm partial to Bisquick. And when you put all that together, you've got to have the stomach of a brain surgeon, I tell you. You can only do it with your hands. You try to make sausage and dry biscuit mix and grated cheese blend together—blend, you understand—it's like getting your daddy and your worthless ex-husband and your best friend at the hairdresser to lie down together naked in the town square of a Sunday afternoon. You got nothing to do but put your hands in it and they end up coated with grease.

This isn't what I'm trying to say, exactly. I am—well, let's face it— a little over forty years old, and I still don't know what happens when I start talking. Do you think I actually want to have a picture in my head of my own flesh-and-blood daddy and my gone-to-seed ex-husband and Ida Mae Pickett, who is the dearest girl in Bovary but maybe also the largest, lying buck naked in the grass under the statue of the South's Defenders? These are thoughts no human being should ought to have. But don't I also know that all three of them aren't near as hurtful to me there in the grass than if they're still talking to me in my head like they can do? Isn't that why when we tell things, they get bigger than life, all bent out of shape? So you can look at them and not have to take them so real?

How many mornings of my life was it just a frying pan and my daddy sitting in his undershirt with his chest hairs sticking out and his sausage patties frying there in front of me. Grease is grease. And so is sausage. Nothing bizarre about that. And my daddy talking in a long unstoppable sizzle of words about how I was too fat and too lazy and too much like my dead mama and too liberal in my thinking and did I get the brand of sausage without the monosodium glutamate this time, he wasn't having anything Chinese in his morning sausage, he was an American and proud of it. My daddy was a difficult man, but he wasn't ignorant. He knew how to read a label on a package and figure out what it meant. As far as I was concerned, if a thing was Chinese and made the flavor better—even of your country sausage—then it was okay. Even Tennessee Pride has that MSG in it, and they're still proud.

And if I just said to Daddy, "This is pure sausage, nothing but," he'd never know the difference anyway, from the taste, except it'd be good, and that's what he wanted. So sometimes I'd feed him the un-American sausage, making sure to throw out the label so he couldn't read it. To tell the truth, I'd rather lie to my daddy than disappoint him in the matter of his sausage. All his life long, he'd eat his breakfast one way. He'd cut the center right out of one of his patties and put it on the side and then eat all his eggs and his grits and his toast and all the other sausage, mixing them up together, wolfing them down, but he'd save that center bite for last. And it all came down to that. I couldn't help myself caring, being who I am. And it's been that way all my life. For a few years, my caring so bad about a thing like that shifted from my daddy to my husband. But he run away to Mobile in pursuit of I don't know what-all and I went back and lived with Daddy for a spell, till he got tired of me in general and he bought me and Eddie our mobile home out on the edge of town. Still, he done that on the condition that weekday mornings I'd continue to make his breakfast before I went in to work. Pretty much till my spaceman lover come into my life, I'd sit at the kitchen table where I grew up and wait till there was nothing left on my daddy's plate but that last bite of sausage and he'd slow way down and then at last he'd spear it with his fork and lift it up, like he was a Catholic, which he wasn't, far from it, but if he was, he would've crossed himself right then, before putting it on his tongue, it was that important to him.

And the sad thing was, till I flew off into outer space for the first time, it was that important for me, too. My daddy'd taken everything else away, to feel good about. You know what I mean? I heard all those words he said. I knew I didn't have much to take pride in. Except that bite of sausage.

Weary now, and sad again, we stop speaking, my wife Edna Bradshaw and I. I am. I am apart. I wish to place my sixteen finger-tips upon her. But her eyes droop shut, and I take her in my hands but I help her to slide down, her body sinking beneath the covers as if this were the sea and she were a pirate ship full of treasure.

5 I wonder sometimes about dreams. There is often music in my head as I sleep, the humming of my blood and my marrow, but there are no sights, no people visiting, no dramas. For the creatures of this planet, there is never any rest. The world they try to leave behind will not let go. It pursues them into the darkest places and unfolds its tent and strings its lights and It's Another Opening of Another Show. Bigtime Thrills and Spills. I listen to these creatures speak of their dreams and I want very badly to bring them peace, to put my hands on all of them and let them sleep, truly sleep, and take their rest. After Edna's night voice was Made Fresh from Pork, Ham, and Pork Loin and Spiced Just Right, she must have begun to *dream* of sausage, as well. And it was a Sausage Dream of great persuasiveness, for in spite of the memories of her father, she wakes after her sleep with the idea of making breakfast for all of our visitors.

I say, "They will each of them sleep for as long as it is convenient for us."

"That's okay," Edna says. "I'll be ready for them—let's see, there's twelve plus you and me—just give me an hour."

"But I wish for most of them to continue to sleep. I must do my work now, speaking to them one at a time."

A sadness passes over Edna's face. I do not understand. And now even a welling of tears. "What is it, my wife Edna Bradshaw? Have I been a clunkhead?"

She smiles at me, though the tears do not seem to cease. "No," she says. "Not at all, Desi. Where'd you even get that word? It's okay. I don't mean to interfere with your work."

"You spoke to me last night of the sadness of making breakfast."

"I did?"

I lift my hand and she remembers. She casts her eyes downward. I think she is embarrassed. "Please," I say. "This was a very interesting thing you told me. But as a consequence, I do not understand why it would disappoint you so, not to do this thing for all these people."

"They need to eat."

"We have always had adequate ways to feed our visitors."

Edna is not looking at me now. Still another mood has come over her. She pulls a tissue from a box beside our bed, and another, and three more quickly, and a sixth and seventh, and then even more, so that I lose count, she is snatching at them as if they are in a place they should not be. Finally she contemplates her hand stuffed full of tissues. She addresses the hand. "I know about how you feed your visitors. I was a visitor once upon a time, don't forget."

I say, "It is a Liquid Diet Rich in Protein and Food Value. You need not worry for them."

Edna pats at her eyes with her handful of tissues. "I do wish we'd begun this conversation before I put my makeup on. This is a real test for my No-Smear Revlon."

"This is a surprising subject suddenly to find in your words," I say.

"Well, you spacemen aren't near as smart as you think you are," my wife Edna Bradshaw says, sharply.

I am having trouble following her associative connections. The disparity I have noted, between the words inside me and the words

I speak, has a corollary. It is this. I can begin to hear the latent music in the words of this world when I can place the voice inside me. But when these words must pass from the voice of a visitor across a physical space and then enter my mind as external things, things that must then be transformed back into spirit, into music, into deep feeling, into the cries of a soul, at these times I think I understand very little. In this sense, certainly, my wife is correct, though I would rephrase her assertion. I am not acting near as smart as I feel I am capable of being. She is watching me now, even as this analysis is passing through me, delaying my audible voice to her. And now I am struck by the sudden realization that I thought of her, implicitly, as a "visitor" moments ago. I was reluctant last night even to characterize her as a *woman* and now she is a *visitor,* which is even farther from my feelings for her. And still nothing presents itself for me to speak. There seem to be no words to send back across this physical space. Will she remember me from this moment as she remembers her father, with regret and anger? Am I failing her in some terrible way even in the very process of wondering if I am failing her in some terrible way? This is a real test for my No-Smear superior intelligence. I am not as smart as I think I am.

And I say, unexpectedly for both of us, "Clunkhead."

Her hand lunges forward and grabs a sizable part of my cheek and squeezes and jiggles it. This physical attack is very distressing to me, especially given the sudden lightheartedness of her demeanor as she does it. This is a side to Edna that shocks me, and the violence goes on. I am bearing it the best I can and now Edna even says, "Oh you spaceman," in that cheery, loving voice that I have grown to recognize in spite of the neutrality of the words themselves. I am very confused and her attack on my cheek ceases and her hand drops and I think I have missed something. I think she has meant this gesture as a friendly thing. After all, she does not have suckers on her fingers. Without recognizing the drastic difference of effect, given the limitations of her species' body, she could be trying to replicate the basic act of physical attachment that I offer her.

"My wife Edna Bradshaw, may I ask if you are feeling angry at your husband in a physically actionable way?"

She pauses briefly with an inward concentration, as if she is translating what I have said. But quite quickly she replies, "I'm not angry, Desi. You clunkhead sweetheart spaceman. I love you." And her hand rushes at my cheek again and grabs that very same handful of flesh and my analysis is, thankfully, confirmed. I bear the pain with patience, for she does not know what it is that she is doing.

Finally she releases me a second time and I turn my fingertips to the task of restoring life to my cheek. She says, "Can I make them breakfast one at a time then, as you choose to wake them up?"

"Of course," I say. "I only wished to protect you from your sadness."

I realize that this declaration has touched Edna and I quickly cover both my cheeks with my hands. But she has already spun around and she disappears into the corridor.

I myself am left not only with an Achy Breaky cheek but the lingering mystery of my wife Edna Bradshaw's willingness, even eagerness, to return to the activity that has been a source of abiding pain in her life. But I ain't stupid, pardner. In spite of its ability to baffle me again and again, this is a pattern I recognize. I have encountered it often before, in many others from this world.

There is a sound in the corridor and I think Edna has returned. I move to the door, eager to see her again, and I open it.

A figure of shadow drops to its knees before me. The face turns up with black lips and a dark, spiky penumbra. It is the young woman named Citrus. Her eyes fix on me and she clasps her hands before her. She cries, "Art thou He that should come? Or look we for another?"

I do not understand her question. I also wonder at her being awake, though from her words she obviously is only partially so. She lifts her clasped hands higher. "Please," she says.

I say, "I know these things are difficult to believe."

And she says, "Art thou the Christ? Tell us."

I pass my hand before her and her eyes close and her body sags and I take her up in my arms and I carry her along the corridor to her dark space and I place her on her bed, on her back, her legs straight, her arms folded on her chest. She will rest now. When it is her time, I will call her forth and she will speak.

6 I am. That is all I know from the beginning of things. I am. That, at least, is a matter of clarity, though the answers to all the questions that follow are not clear at all. Those are matters of philosophy. Of music. Of the Great Mysteries. And yet I must try to divine answers to many of those abiding questions, at least about this complex and alien world, so that I can do what I must and in doing so not create such confusion as to cast a whole world down. Many will look upon me and be sore afraid.

And I am alone in this task. It is reasoned that one spaceman—I would add, a *clunkhead* spaceman, at that—may not seem to be so great a threat. I hover above a vast place with billions of individual sentiences speaking trillions of words every day in an attempt to move beyond the one matter of ontological clarity. The *I am.* Though, incidentally, there are some on my home planet who would challenge even that first principle as a settled matter. But if they were sincere in their skepticism, they would find it both meaningless and impossible even to express the challenge. Who would they think they are sending their thoughts to? Or, even, who would they think are the entities having those thoughts? If there were but one imperiously great and brutally wise sentience in a meaningless universe, it would never let on for a moment.

I am. A clunkhead. Drugged by words. Hooked on them. Infected by them, as a visitor to a foreign place is infected by a virus for which he has no defenses. Shaken by them. Unbalanced by them. Made delirious by them. Enrapt by them. Transformed by them. Filled full of false and, it seems, endlessly renewable hopes for them. I sit with a new voice waiting in the panel before me. The speaker—the man who drove the bus—has returned to his sleep, though with a delicious and nutritious country breakfast in his stomach. Edna brought it in when the interview was finished and he ate it before both of us, gratefully, at ease with us, even when my wife Edna Bradshaw said to him, "If you really want a pony-tail, I wish you'd let me sit you down and do something a little cuter with it." I held this voice once, as it first found words, but that is hardly sufficient. I move my hand to put the voice inside me once more, put it inside me in solitude. I am Henry Gillette. *Call me Hank. I'm not afraid of that, though I'm always meeting guys who'd much rather me be Henry. But I've never been a Nelly, even for an evening, even for just the sport of it, even when I was going through that early teenage thing when it was clear I wasn't going to fit the profile of a real man in America. That was at the end of the bad old fifties. It wasn't easy.*

But my mother's clothes, for instance, never did have an allure for me, though I've always appreciated it in my lovers, those who had that sweet soft edge to them. Me being inclined to walk without rolling my shoulders and wiggling my butt—I think it just made me love all the more those guys who were natural like that. Some of my friends, when I say things like this, they think I'm overcompensating. Gay men don't have to be one thing or another, they'd say. There's plenty of us in leather and studs and also in tailored suits or football pads or Arrow shirts and chinos and they never vamp at all. Never. The Lady—meaning me— doth protest too much, making this point so strongly.

Maybe they're right. Maybe there's part of me I'm just trying to make be still. But I don't think so. I am what I am. When I realized I was gay, it was just a matter of how I wanted to express the feeling of love. When I loved somebody, loved the way the person spoke or thought or looked, then the part of their body that was hidden became like a se-cret, it took on a kind of magic, it became more than itself, it became a way to touch not only their body but everything else they were. But when I started feeling love like that, the male parts could take on the magic for me and the female parts couldn't. It was as simple as that. All pussies looked alike, and every cock was wonderfully, specially different, as dif-ferent as a voice or a personality.

My Adam—that's what we used to call our first male sexual part-ner—didn't come along for a few years. I kept my feelings to myself. Being who I am, nobody ever guessed. So I went off to Northwestern University in the fall of 1963, and this was a good school, I was pretty smart, and my parents lived in Chicago and I was just an El ride away from them. But I did stay in a dorm, way up on the north edge of the campus. My room-mate was from Pittsburgh. His name was George. We slept in the same room, an arm's length away from each other across the narrow floor, and we never knew about each other. Not for nearly three months. That's how scared everybody was back then, or naive. When we went down to the shower at the end of the hall, we both hid in our terry-cloth robes, from each other and especially from all the others on the floor, and we didn't dare let our eyes wander, for fear of being found out.

Then the thing nobody ever dreamed of suddenly happened and I was in a lecture hall when it did, watching slides of nebulae and spiral galaxies and dying stars. Our professor was named Hynek and he had a pointed gray goatee and thick glasses and he'd won me over right away. I was going to major in astronomy. He was also an adviser to the Air Force about UFOs, and I liked that, too. There was a whole other kind of creature in the universe, there was a distant world where things were drastically different from what everybody thought was right and nor-mal. Needless to say, I liked the idea of that.

I was sitting up near the top of the hall. A great spiraling splash of stars was on the screen and we were understanding how birth and death were going on all the time on an unimaginably vast scale and then it was time to go and Professor Hynek stacked his notes, which was our sign, though it was hard to say, set against the issues we'd just considered, how such an unimaginably small gesture should have any effect on anything. But there was that end-of-a-class shuffling sound all over the place and we were back on the planet Earth and then a voice was at the door behind us and it said, "The President's been shot."

    I didn't go to the dorm for a long while. I knew he was going to die, though it wasn't quite official yet. I went down to the little beach at the south end of campus, where Sheridan Road takes a jog toward the lake. Nobody was there. I hunched up against the iron jetty and squeezed my eyes shut and filled myself with the smells of rust and dead alewives and there was thunder out to the east, out at the razor cut of the horizon, and there was another smell, the ozone off the lake, which was a thing you knew was big, just from the smell of it, as big as a galaxy. And for a moment I thought to open my eyes and face that horizon and walk out into the lake and just keep walking until it overwhelmed me.

    I didn't expect this. I never thought I was suicidal. But things were suddenly clarified. You look through the eye of a telescope or the glory hole of a john wall and it all comes down to the same thing. You're a gathering of atoms swirling around some kind of center and you never chose any of it, neither the swirl nor the center, and when you focus your eye you might find a similar body to yours here and there, but there's light years in between. I loved Jack Kennedy. I didn't even know that till his beautiful shaggy head was blown apart. I still had never even touched a man, and now I felt a passionate love rush on me hand in hand with death. I was being prepared for the last two decades of the century and the great plague, I suppose. But at the time, without the solace of a single remembered embrace, I could only open my eyes and step to the shore and look out at the lake and very seriously consider putting all this behind me.

*Then George was suddenly by my side. "I wondered if it was you,"
he said.*

*I wasn't surprised at all that he was here. I said, "I want to be holding
him in my arms, right now, cradling his head and telling him good-bye."*

*And George said, "That smarmy Bouvier girl in the pillbox hat
doesn't have a clue what he needs."*

*We didn't speak another word. You'd think there would've had to
be a clearer declaration between us, since we'd missed signs that were
surely even more obvious about each other all along. But we'd made our
way to the moment that most gays do, and sometimes it comes on you in
an instant. You go from seeing only darkness to having a very subtle
perception of light.*

*George and I walked back up to the dorm, and with the other men
of Elder Hall we watched Walter Cronkite weep and Lyndon Johnson—
the cow—take over the country, and then, without a further word, we
went back to our room and fully became what we had always been.*

I sit with these words for a time. I try always to set aside the
ways of my own world, the issues of my own life. My task, of ne-
cessity, is to submerge myself in this planet Earth. But I do reflect
for a moment on the often rigorous and heavily sanctioned taboos
of physical affection in this place. The mores are different on my
home planet. Even there, however, I, Desi the Spaceman, am clearly
a Manly Man, Fresh as an Irish Spring with a Lot to Like—Filter,
Flavor, and a Flip-top Box—and I am a Hero of the Beach whose
body will bring me Fame Instead of Shame and whose Lust is for
Life. These things are true of me in light of this planet Earth's public declarations of value that I have found in my collected records
of printed matter and in my scanning tapes of the endless trans-
missions filling the air. Though it is also true that my man's body
is a very skinny one to the Earthman's eye. But I am certainly not
a ninety-seven-pound weakling. I am a seventy-eight-pound

Powerhouse of Strength and Vigor. And though the female coun-
terparts on my home planet are exceedingly skinny, too, I am
sufficiently in tune, in some instinctive way, with Red-blooded
American Male Values so as to have acquired a sincere and intense
appreciation for knockers.

But listen to me. I have set aside the values of my species so
effectively, given my mission here, that the Lady (meaning me, in
this context, Desi the Spaceman) Doth Protest Too Much. On my
home planet I would never dream of spending all these words on
establishing my masculinity—not that we have *words* there—
though we can be subject to a similar psychological syndrome with
our transmitted thoughts—not that I am really guilty of that either, given the relevance of the premise of my masculinity to the
larger point I wish to make—a point, by the way, which still remains unmade—and listen to me again, I am beginning to sound
like my wife Edna Bradshaw now, digressing into clarification
after clarification—even in *that* clarification, as a matter of fact—
though it wasn't *clarifying* anything exactly, more like amplifying
or even digressing—which is a trait of hers, as well, and one that
just as inexorably carries her away from her main point—just as I
continue to do now, as these words—quite alarmingly—come
unbidden, as they seem veritably to choose themselves.

I leap up from where I sit and I sing a thin, clear note of frus-
tration at full voice. Our New and Improved Tracking Lights cannot even follow me quickly enough and my face is shrouded in
darkness for a moment. This reminds me of sleep. My own sleep.
I am fortunate that all my studies of this planet have not affected
my sleep. I still dream only in music. There is a place where the
words cannot follow me. This is a comfort.

The light finds me. I can wave it away, but I do not. I am all
right now. I am determined to reassert some measure of power over

these words. I have so adamantly established the premise of my masculinity in order to emphasize that in spite of that masculinity, as a member of the primary species on my planet I am free to give the beats of my heart through my fingertips—which is the most intimate of our physical sensations—to anyone, without cultural stigma. I could do so with a male as readily as a female. There are other, gender-defining parts of our bodies, and certainly they are effective in reproduction only in certain prescribed ways, but the pleasure of their use in interpersonal communication is not seen as a matter subject to cultural restraints—unless, of course, made exclusive by a formalized commitment. They are surface parts, after all. And even with the deepest part, the truly hidden part, the most intimate part, we acknowledge no limitation in its sharing. We can choose to share our hearts with anyone.

I realize that a meditation like this is a dangerous distraction. It is not my own kind that I must come to understand. When I descend from this machine, a solitary spaceman, to bring, in the vision of my body, the central message of the universe to this place that has lived too long in cosmic loneliness, I must know who it is that will look upon me. They do not have hands like mine. They cannot freely give the beating of their hearts.

And now my wife Edna Bradshaw rushes into the room, the tracking lights flaring upon her, her face tight from concern. "I heard you scream," she says. She is before me now, her hands fluttering as if they feel their own genetic inadequacy.

"I sang." I do not wish to raise these complex issues with my quick-to-worry Edna and so I offer not a lie but an incomplete truth.

"Does that pass for singing where you come from?" Edna asks, and I do not hear even a trace of suspicion in her. She is simply filled with fascination and wonder. Her Enquiring Mind Wants to

Know. I put my hands upon her bare arms. I give her my heart, pulse beat by pulse beat, taking pleasure in who she is.

"Oh you spaceman," she says and she draws nearer and puts her arms around me.

Though my species is free to give love to anyone, I feel very happy, holding my wife Edna Bradshaw, that I am who I am.

She turns her face and lays her head on my chest and says, "Desi, you know I'm not the kind of woman who is always prying into her hubby's work."

She pauses as if for me to affirm that I do in fact know this assertion to be true. I try to understand her. She has used a word that is unfamiliar to me. I say, "Am I the hubby?"

"Yes, my sweet spaceman, you are the hubby in the picture. Of course, this was true of me with my previous husband as well. I would not pry. I am not a prier. As you may recall my saying, he was a telephone installer, and I always declined to inquire about his wires and his receivers and his clicky hold buttons and so forth."

"And you have continued this policy with your spaceman hubby. Yes, I can affirm this to be true of you."

Edna burrows closer to me. She says, "But now that I'm seeing firsthand how you talk to my fellow Earth people, and since I'm kind of helping out, welcoming them and cooking for them and so forth, it's sort of like I'm working *with* you, wouldn't you say?"

Before I am able even to comprehend her question—my mind is always lagging her words by a few moments—Edna goes on, "Even if you wouldn't say it like that exactly, we are coming to the close of the century, if you don't mind my saying so, and though my daddy taught me to act certain ways and though there were similar certain ways that folks in Bovary always thought were the right ways for a wife to act, I've been taking some mighty big leaps with you, Desi darling, more or less strictly on faith, and I just need to ask you this one thing about your work. Do you have some kind of master plan here for the human race? That is, for the folks on Earth, 'cause you certainly seem real human to me. Of course you do. I'm talking a little stupid now. I don't mean to suggest you're not part of, well, the human race. But you *are* a spaceman. And you're doing all this interviewing and studying and you do have all these wonderful and pretty scary machines. I'm running on at the mouth now. I know that. But it's because I'm just a little bit nervous about all this. You know?"

And now she stops speaking and pulls back from me far enough so that she can look into my face and finally await an answer. My mind has fallen far behind. But she is keeping silent, letting me catch up. I say, "We spacemen wish to understand." I want that to be sufficient, but Edna continues to wait. I say, "We go here and there, as a species. We listen, we watch." Again, I wish to reveal no more.

But Edna, for all her self-deprecation, is smart. And I am her husband. Even with her species' characteristic lack of telepathy, she often senses true things about me, things I sometimes am only barely aware of myself. She knows I am being evasive. I try to think how to phrase a further revelation to her. But before I can speak, she begins again.

"I guess I did actually pry a couple of times, with my ex-husband," she says. "Well, not pry, exactly, because I had fit reason to ask a few questions. He came home from work one lunchtime, and I had made him a Baloney Surprise, which I don't have to go into, but it is a surprise, I can tell you, and a very pleasant one. But he wasn't saying much and I happen to look out in the driveway and it seems he's not driving his telephone-company truck any more. He's driving a cable-TV truck. I did ask some questions that day and got some answers I probably could've done without, except I had to know sometime that he was going to leave me so he could fulfill his lifelong dream of participating in the fast-growing and exciting business of cable TV, leaving behind his job that involved the same old telephones day in and day out. Is it something like that?"

She hesitates again. "Something like what?" I say, and I ask this from a genuine state of confusion.

Edna replies, "Like I really need to know and I'm probably going to find out anyway sooner or later but I'm going to get mighty uncomfortable with the answer and wish it was later?"

I say, "I am devoted to you, my wife Edna Bradshaw."

"Well, that's good," Edna says. "That's the most important thing. Course, the destiny of the whole planet Earth is pretty important, too. But I love you, Desi, and I know you wouldn't hurt a fly."

I wish to put my wife's mind even further at ease but suddenly, beyond her, in the doorway, a silhouette appears, an unexpected visitor, the lights rush to the spot and once again it is the young woman called Citrus, and she lifts her arms above her head and she makes a sound that I presume passes for singing where she comes from and Edna starts and screams and Citrus undulates into the room, her arms waving above her as if they are growing on the ocean floor.

7 I think, as the young woman who calls herself Citrus falls on her knees before me, that my appearance on the eve of this planet's millennium will come with the effect of a Baloney Surprise. No, perhaps I am wrong about that, for though my wife Edna Bradshaw said the dish was a great *surprise*—as I imagine it surely must be, knowing both the substance and the cook in question—and in this, my analogy is apt enough—she also said the surprise was a *pleasant* one. Of that, concerning my mission, I am quite doubtful, even for those like Citrus, who is now clutching at my legs and crying "Hosanna in the highest." She is not afraid. She is not hostile. But somehow this does not seem Baloney Surprise–like for Citrus. She is in a state of extremity that surely is not pleasant for her. I am anxious to hear her true voice.

Edna bends to her. "Honey, now get on up. You've got your hands on my husband's cute little boney legs and I'm going to get jealous in a minute here."

Citrus suddenly looks Edna square in the face, making my wife shrink back from her. "He has come," Citrus says.

"Honey, we've got to get rid of that black lipstick and that spiky hair. I'll be happy to give you a Mary-Lou's-Southern-Belle-Beauty-Nook special for free if you just get up now."

I say to my wife, "I believe there is a significant residue of recreational drugs still in her system. This is why she cannot sleep. It may also account for her mistaken impression of your spaceman husband."

Edna whispers to me, loudly, "I'd say there's a significant residue of church in this girl, as well, Desi honey."

"Holy holy holy holy," Citrus says.

"I've always been a churchgoing woman, more or less," Edna says.

"Hallelujah," Citrus says.

"But I've got to tell you, the folks in Bovary who'd be most dead-set against my marrying you would be the churchgoing folks, if they knew the true facts of my disappearance."

Citrus, who has prostrated herself before me, rises suddenly up high on her knees, the light flashing on the metal studs and rings which pierce her face and ears, and she lifts her arms, her hands blooming in reverent supplication before my face. She cries, "Praise God. Thank you for your Son who you have allowed me to gaze upon."

"This girl needs to lie down," Edna says.

I say, "Perhaps it is time for her delicious country breakfast."

At this idea, Edna lifts her hands high before her, palms up. For a moment she and Citrus share what appears to be the same gesture, though they are surely in quite different states of mind. Edna says, "I am such a fool. And a bad hostess to boot. Keep an eye on this poor girl while I go get her what she needs to fix her up."

Edna rushes away and I am left with a renewed outpouring of reverence from this mouth that I must admit scares me. I am not used to lips in general, but this blackened slash of a mouth—this deep-space rift that is compulsively shaping *words*—is particularly frightening for me, its apparent conviction of my beneficent importance notwithstanding. Perhaps Citrus does indeed need a makeover from the cosmetological wisdom of Bovary, Alabama. Though her boyfriend seemed quite devoted to her in our Welcome-to-the-Spaceship Party. But I share my wife Edna Bradshaw's concern with Citrus's chosen appearance.

She falls forward again on her face, crying. "Lord, I will wash your feet with my hair."

"Please," I say, bending now and taking her by the arms. Though I do not give her my heartbeat through my fingertips. I merely pull at her, and she goes quite heavy in my hands, straining downward.

"Oh my," she says. "All these toes. So many toes."

Like the fingers on my hands, there are eight toes on each of my feet, exposed now, from my casual interviewing attire, in the very largest-sized flip flops.

"Of course," she cries. "Of course, Lord, you are blessed with toes, your toes are multiplied according to your righteousness." And she strains harder, saying, "I will wash your feet with my hair like the sinner woman at the house of the Pharisee."

And my hands lose their grip and she dips her head and sharp pains begin to bite and bite at me. I look. Her hair is as black as her lips and done into lacquered spikes. These poke and poke at my feet.

"Please," I say, trying again to pull her up. I am very strong for my species, which, pound for pound, is notably stronger than the primary species of this planet, but I am struggling with this woman's ardor. I say, "Please. Your hair is not suited for the task you have given it," and at last I am succeeding in pulling her away, though she continues to strive to thrash her head against my feet.

She says, "I'm not worthy, Lord. It's true." And she abruptly yields completely. As if our gravitation devices have suddenly failed, she rises up quickly at my efforts, and now she is standing before me. Her eyes search my face. "I didn't know God had so many toes."

I say, "That is an issue for which I can offer no insight. I am certain, however, that you have insufficient evidence of God's toes by numbering mine."

I have confused her with my words. She is staring hard into my face. I wave my hand between us. I wave it again over her head. She sighs and closes her eyes and opens them and her eyes widen and she says, "What the fuck?"

I believe that I have revived her.

"Miss Citrus," I say, for that is her chosen name at this level of consciousness.

"Oh my God," she says.

For a moment, with her renewed invocation of a deity, I think she has slipped back once again to her twilight state. But, as this world's words so often do, hers slip away from their apparent meaning, for she adds, "You look like a fucking spaceman."

"More precisely, a *standing* spaceman."

She jerks backward, begins to look frantically around her. I wave my hand once more between us and she grows calm. She is ready to speak now.

I call her by her official name, which I have learned in full from her Texas driver's license. "Judith Marie Nash," I say.

And she acknowledges this name. "Yes?" she says.

"Please sit here." I motion to the visitor's chair in the center of the room. It is already bathed in a soft white light. She moves to it without further urging and she turns and sits. I go to my place before her and sit in the shadows.

"Please now," I say. "Speak to me."

And I am Judith Marie Nash. *I used to dream about the nails in Jesus' hands and feet. Not the way my daddy would have me dream, I'm sure. My daddy is a man of God. My daddy would take his Bible and it was bound in beautiful calf-skin leather and the paper was so thin and crinkly and yet so strong that not a page of it was torn no matter how many times somebody had rushed through looking for the Word, the Holy Word, but he would take his Bible and hold it up when my brother and me and my mama was sitting around the living room with him and we were all doing our prayers and our studying, he'd hold it up high. And that Bible, full of God's Holy Word, would droop in his hand, it would just go limp over his fingers, the thick shaft of pages, the two page-marker ribbons dangling down. It was so supple. So supple and skin-smooth. And I would have these thoughts. And they would seem to come straight from the mouth of God, straight from His Word. This Bible being held up like that felt like a real private thing. I mean a private thing about a man's body. You know the thing I mean. I don't know why, when I'm talking about how I grew up and all, that I start feeling the taboos again about these words—I mean, of course, a man's cock. I knew—part of me knew—that it was a terrible thing I was thinking. But another part of me thought it was all right. And it wasn't like the part that felt it was all right was the future me, the me that my father would be expecting to go straight to hell. It was the me still believing in the Holy Word. Because every word was true in that book. Every one. True like cosmic true. True in your soul and in the marrow of your bones and true by every hair on your head, which are all numbered by God—you can read that in Matthew chapter ten verse thirty. And, of course, every other hair is numbered, too. How could anything escape the notice of God? He put hair on your head and he also put it around your cock, if you're a guy, or your pussy, of course, if you're a girl, and they've got to all be numbered, too, those hairs. So the fact that the Bible in my daddy's hand made me think of a guy's cock, it seemed right to me, by the Book.*

Just consider King David. How beloved he was by God. How great he was in God's eyes. How God loved him to go out and deal with the bodies of Israel's enemies. Because in the Word, which is true for all eternity—my own father taught that as the cornerstone of everything else—in the first book of Samuel in the Bible David fell in love with the daughter of Saul, who was beloved, as well, being made the first King of Israel by God as prophesied by Samuel, and David loved Saul's daughter and what did he bring as a dowry for her? He brought the foreskins off the cocks of two hundred Philistines. He did. You can look it up in First Samuel chapter eighteen. I dreamed about that for a long while, too, even while I was awake. When I daydreamed of my own wedding, blessed by its true Bible-based holiness, and my daddy giving me away to a godly Christian boy, I dreamed of a dowry like this marriage that God had brought to his beloved David. I saw a great black case of fine, supple, calf-skin leather, and it would be opened, and there they would be, laid out on blue velvet inside, those wonderful intimate pieces of flesh off the cocks of two hundred boys. Mostly the boys at Sam Houston High School in Waco, Texas, where I was a sophomore when I first started having this dream.

Of course, my daddy couldn't deal with the literal truth of that God-approved dowry of foreskins. He believed the things it was convenient for him to believe. Like the earth is six thousand years old. That was real important to him for some reason. But ask him why if a man is wounded in his testicles he's cast out of the church, which is true forever and ever amen from the book of Deuteronomy chapter twenty-three, and you won't get real clear answers from him, even though, as the father in the family, he's God's direct representative with divine inspiration—that's in the Bible, too, somewhere, and he wouldn't let us forget it, but a guy who gets in an accident and his balls get hurt, why he has to be cast out of God's house is something my daddy refuses to address. He even took my Bible away from me for asking. But my daddy put his own balls in a wringer over that. He wanted me to study the Bible so that I'd be a worthy daughter of a Godly man like him, which everybody in Waco knew about him. But how could I do that if he had my Bible? So he had to give it back to me and then he put me under threat of hell not to read certain parts of the One and Only Holy Book of the Creator of the Universe, literally true in every word. But then there was the guy that God got real pissed at and smote dead just because he touched the ark of the covenant when he was only trying to keep it from falling on the ground when the oxen that was pulling the cart it was on stumbled. Course my daddy would say that God could get killingly angry at anybody He chose to and nobody could question that, because He's God. And the same goes for God's direct representative in every family on Earth. Him, for example, my daddy.

And then I read in the Bible that if a son—and you can imagine they wouldn't go any easier on a daughter, harder if anything—if a son doesn't obey his parents, even just to eat too much and drink too much, then the parents are supposed to take him to the elders and have the son stoned to death. This is what God wants, according to his Holy Word. I sure wasn't going to ask my daddy about that one. I'm sure he'd checked that out already and was irritated at Big Government for making that kind of holy justice pretty hard to get away with these days. These days being the corrupt End Times, of course. A disobedient child would be even worse than those kids who went up in smoke, and Daddy didn't shed any tears for them, knowing how True and Beautiful was the judgment of God.

We went out to Overlook Hill next to the intersection of State 340 and Farm 2491 so we could watch that Branch Davidian cult in their compound after they'd barricaded themselves up and were holding off the FBI and all. Not really watch. It took binoculars to see anything from there and we just brought our Bibles and our "Forwarding Address: Hell" tracts. There was probably some closer place to go, but this was close enough for Daddy, and for a bunch of others, too, because there was all types on the hill. The place was crammed full of those making their righteousness clear to the world as a testament and those acting in sin from their unrighteousness, supporting this cult and its Satan-controlled leader.

And there was a bunch of others in between, press people and picnickers and people selling T-shirts and gimme caps and hot dogs and stuff. I wandered away in between prayers and used my own little bit of money when I got hungry and had a Koresh Burger, which was cooked over charcoal by a guy wearing a "WACO—We Ain't Coming Out" T-shirt, and it maybe was the best-tasting hamburger I've ever had in my life and I was loving it till my father saw me and he came and grabbed this meal conceived in unrighteousness out of my hand and gave me a stoning-by-the-elders look and he threw the Koresh Burger down on the ground and crushed it under his heel. There's nothing in the Bible about littering, as far as I know, so this wasn't either here or there in terms of his witnessing to the world, from my daddy's point of view. But he was ready to do me in, as a true witness to God's word, right there and then, if only this was the sort of times when that was possible, but lucky for me it's the wicked End Times instead. So he grabbed me hard by the arm and dragged me back and put me on my knees next to my always-faithful brother and my daddy started to pray for the Triumph of Jesus over the wickedness of the world as was clearly represented by those people hiding and sinning in that cult compound right here in Waco. My daddy may even have started talking in tongues or something because I stopped hearing any sense in his words at all. He was saying things like hunga marunga adenoid hallelujah. Everyone we know at church and at a lot of churches in Waco would say these were inspired words my daddy was saying, he was filled with the Holy Spirit. But as far as I was concerned he was just fading farther and farther away from me, at that time.

And then it was the next Monday about noon and I was eating maybe the worst-tasting hamburger I've ever had in my life, in our school cafeteria, and thinking about that hamburger on Overlook Hill, when there was a big stir and we all went out to the parking lot and off in the distance, out to the northeast of town in the direction of the Branch Davidians, there was a pillar of smoke as dark as the worst grime you've ever seen, like the color of those people's souls, I thought, and as soon as I did, I knew that thought came from my daddy, how he saw the world.

And that night at the dinner table my daddy prayed to God in praise of how He'd shown us all in this family the true path and saved us from hell where every last one of those folks who'd burned up today was going to feel the fiery wrath of God for all eternity.

And I said, What about the children?

And he said, They have been brought to perdition by their parents. Don't you think there was children in Sodom when the fires came down from heaven and no one was saved except Lot and his two daughters and even his wife was turned into a pillar of salt?

And will you pass me some? I said. Salt, that is.

And my daddy did and I put it on my hamburger which my mama had made and which tasted pretty bad, it needed more salt than I could give it, but I shook the salt out and I thought of the body of Lot's wife making things taste good long after she was dead.

And I was wondering: If the fires ever were to come down in Waco, on everybody, not just the Branch Davidians, would God first send his angels to the house of this true and faithful servant of the Lord, my daddy, and say, Go, take your wife and your son and your daughter and go from this Waco, for it is full of iniquity and will be destroyed, even the women and the children? And I looked at my daddy then and if the answer was no, God wouldn't do that for this man, then my daddy was full of shit all along about what was right and holy and what wasn't. And if the answer was yes, if God was such that He'd pull the four of us out of here and burn up all the rest and send them to hell for eternity, then that wasn't a God I should give a good fuck about. That's what I realized right there and then.

So I went off. I made my plan and Daddy never knew about it till I was gone, but the night before I was hitting the road, he came to my room and knocked real soft and I said, Come in, and he sat on the side

*of my bed and he said, Honey, I know we have our differences. I know I
seem real hard on you sometimes. But I just want you to know that it's
because I love you. I care about your happiness, not just today and tomorrow but forever.*

*My daddy says this real soft and he pats my hand and he goes out
without trying to wring any promises or anything from me.*

*But these were just words, really. Just words. Since then, I've thought
about the words that weren't there in what he said and could never be
there.*

Like: I guess the children are okay, the ones that got burnt up.

*Or: Certain things just don't make sense to me either about who
God is or what He really wants.*

*And I've thought about the words that weren't there in what he said
but you could hear them lurking outside my door in the hall ready to
jump back in his mouth as soon as he left.*

*Like: I may seem hard but this is the way the God of the Universe
wants me to be, so too bad.*

Or: We may have our differences but I'm always right.

*Or: I love you, but I'd be ready in a second to offer your life up—
or in these wimpy times at least just cast you out of the family—if I figure you're lost to God's Word as I see it.*

*My daddy still had all that in him and on that night he didn't say
anything to contradict it, but in spite of my knowing all the shit things he
simply wasn't saying aloud, I lay there in the dark after he'd gone and I
started weeping and quaking and wishing he meant those other things
that could never be. I guess it was the pat on the hand or just the tone of
his voice or something, and I knew those things were as empty as his
words, they were gestures intended for himself, testifying to what a gentle
and understanding father he was when in fact he wasn't anything like
that. But still I trembled and wept and then I got angry at myself about*

it because I knew the truth. I trembled like the tail of our tabby cat when he's taking a shit, but I couldn't quite get Daddy out of my system. Not till the next morning. That's when I went out the door and only I knew what I was going to do and as soon as I hit the end of the driveway, I was fine and I've never looked back.

And I started dreaming about Jesus, about the nails in His hands and His feet and how I felt about that, how close I felt to Him over those nails, even though part of me was ready to throw the baby Jesus out with my daddy's bathwater. And I felt a man's body-thing about Jesus at that, as terrible as that sounds. It's like something I've learned later, in the places I've lived in and from the people I've been with. You put metal through your flesh and it's a real intimate thing, is what I've learned. And it really feels like that to me. You say, My body will give way for this hard, sharp thing, you can push a metal thing right through me and there it sits, touching me inside my flesh all the time. You can look at it and you can touch it and you can think about it and you're looking at and touching and thinking about the inside of my body, where I'm really living and where usually it's impossible for any other person to get into. But with these rings and these studs and these nails and spikes, some-body else can flow right on inside me, he can be in here with me. And when I found my boyfriend Jared and he found me we just knew that these were things that we had to do with our bodies together. And I knew it was about Jesus, too, from my dreams, though I've never said that to Jared. Not my daddy's Jesus. My own personal Jesus.

Judith Marie Nash who calls herself Citrus falls silent and my own voice falls silent, too, for she was in me and I was in her, as if her words and my voice were nail and flesh. And her eyes fill with tears, as often happens with my wife Edna Bradshaw, and with so many of the beings on this planet. Tears are unknown to my spe-cies. But I find them to be wonderful things, much more direct and honest than these endless words, and they taste of the vast oceans of this place, which I know from the offer of my wife to kiss her cheek which was wet with tears on our wedding night, tears she said were prompted by joy. But these tears in Citrus's eyes are not from joy, I know, and I must acknowledge that even these fragments of the sea are filled with complexity and ambiguity on this planet. They spill over now, Citrus's tears, and I am moved to Reach Out and Touch Someone. Earlier I had touched Citrus without giving her my heart. Now I lay my hands on hers and I let my heart go, I let it enter her with each beat, and she looks down at this in wonder.

Then she lifts her face again to me and she says, "Are you Jesus come again?" She is perfectly clearheaded now.

"No," I say. "I am a spaceman."

And she says, "If the Word is not a literal thing but still a holy thing, then perhaps it was you who was prophesied to come."

This is an alarming idea. "I would know, wouldn't I?"

Citrus looks at our hands again. "Perhaps not."

I feel her longing now, very strongly, as if her heart is beating back into me in return. "I am . . ." I say only this and fall silent.

"Yes," she says, as if I have completed the thought.

I struggle on with words. "I am no one," I say.

"I can feel your sacred heart," she says, still staring at our hands.

And at this moment there is a thump at the door and my wife Edna Bradshaw has flung it open with her foot. She is standing there, silhouetted by the light from the corridor, one foot up, both her hands holding a tray full of Citrus's breakfast.

"Are you done?" she asks.

I gently disengage my hands from Citrus's and she makes a soft sound of understanding and disappointment and yearning and sadness and hope and even more feelings than that, all of which are only diminished and distorted by the naming of them with these words, for they truly exist only in the beating of a heart and a calf-skin book drooping in a hand and twin nipple rings and a grilled hamburger on a hilltop and a black slash of a mouth and a pillar of dark smoke and a planet three-quarters covered with tears.

8 Citrus has taken her breakfast from my wife without rising from the place where she spoke to me and she has eaten it with the tray on her lap. She has the most meticulous of manners about her eating, having cut her Spicy, Finger-Lickin'-Good sausage into tiny morsels, which she chewed carefully and separately from her eggs, which she kept separate from her grits, which she kept separate from her biscuit, a time for each thing and each thing in its own time, and each morsel was carefully attended to without a trace left on her mouth, which she gently dabbed with her paper napkin. And she never licked her fingers, and I was grateful for that, as anyone observing my species and the significance of our fingertips might easily understand. I sensed in Citrus's table manners the influence of her father, though I think she herself was unaware of this connection, given her careful dissociation from him in her body and her words.

My wife Edna Bradshaw stood nearby and watched Citrus eat, her own mouth occasionally opening and biting and chewing faintly as this young woman consumed her food, as if Edna, as well, were part of a species from a distant galaxy, and her mission—like mine in regards to the speaking of words—was to observe the inhabitants of this planet in the eating of food, so that their mastication and hers could become one, as a path to understanding.

When Citrus was finished, Edna took up the tray from Citrus's lap and she said, "Feeling better, honey?"

Citrus nodded yes and I asked her to return with me to her place on the spaceship and she complied without my even having to wave my hand. Edna gave me a knowing nod, which I did not completely understand, as I guided Citrus out the door.

And Edna's nod lingered in my head as Citrus and I moved along the corridors, and now we enter her cubicle and Citrus asks, "Am I to sleep?"

"It is best," I say. "This process is full of stress for your species."

"Will I ever see Jared again?"

"Why should you doubt that?" I ask, though I mean it not as a question but as a declaration of reassurance. I have learned this particular strangeness of Earth words over the years. Sometimes a question is meant as a statement. Sometimes a statement is meant as a question. For example, "I care about your happiness" can mean, "Will you ever learn to follow my plan for you?" Which, however, though a question, can mean, "I cannot imagine you ever turning out the way I want." Which, though a statement, can mean, "Will you lead me to cast you away?" Which can mean, though a question, its own answer: "Yes." These are the times when even my own Extra-Strength brain can grow confused.

Waving her hand before her softly, widely, as if she were trying to send *me* off to sleep, Citrus says, "What if all this is the true meaning of Paul's words in his first letter to the Thessalonians when he prophesies that those in God's church will be caught up together with those who have died in Jesus—caught up *in the clouds, to meet the Lord in the air?*"

She pauses, looking into my eyes intently, a rare thing for a being from this planet, for my eyes are not easy to accept, they are so large, they are so deep, by this planet's standards, but she looks into them as if she is ready to see me for what I am without fear. And what am I in this place? I grow stiff-fingered at the thought of that question, which Citrus inevitably makes me address. And her question is not a question. I have caught her and others up in the clouds and she is meeting me in the air and she is convinced that she understands all of that in a way fraught with eschatological meaning.

"Jared is here too," I say.

"Cool," she says. "Oh that's cool."

"But this is not . . ." I begin and then pause, for I do not know how to address her intense belief.

"It says the dead in Christ have been taken up first. . . . You have the dead here, too, don't you?" She is saying that she knows I do.

And I am led to consider in what sense this might be true. I think of Minnie Butterworth and of Whiplash Willie Jones and of Herbert Jenkins who thought I was a hep cat in my zoot suit, and of many others, all dead and buried on their tiny fragment of cosmic rock but alive still in me, in my voice joined with theirs. Metaphorically, that is. For my species also dies. The individuals of all species everywhere in the known universe die. I know what this means. Or, more precisely, I know how little any being knows of what this means.

But living here in the midst of the clouds in this world full of words and passions, I am moved to understand things in new ways. I feel that those individuals I have known here who have died are still alive in more than a metaphorical way, more than as a construct of *words*. They are real inside me, moving about. Speaking. I hear their voices, even without the aid of my machines. These individual beings are very much alive, in my head and in my place of song and in the very pulse of my fingertips.

"You do, don't you?" she says.

"Do?"

"The dead are taken up here. They are alive here in the clouds."

"Yes," I say.

"Hallelujah."

But I must be honest. I say, "In a sense."

She does not take up this qualification. She says, "I will sleep, Lord. Thy will, not mine, be done." Citrus lies down on her bed, which is notched into the softly glowing walls in this space that I worry now is not sufficient for her, or for any of my visitors. But she seems not to mind. The feeling in me, however, remains. I want to make things good for her. I sit beside her on the edge of her bed. I pat her hand. I wish to use words that will reassure her, give her the hopefulness about the universe that she seeks. In short, I wish to lie. But she and I have our differences on this subject. What is true, if I speak it, will seem hard on her. Still, I find myself caring about Judith Marie Nash's happiness. I pat her hand some more. I could say these things now that are true: her view of the world is still being directed by her father; I am simply a spaceman. But I remain silent for the moment. Happiness, on this planet, is fragile and fleeting. There are so many souls here, yearning, and I myself yearn to touch them all, to give them peace. But I am simply a spaceman. I am.

There is the sound of a rapid, fleshy fluttering in the room. I look down. I am still patting her hand. At a drastically brisk pace, it seems. I am unaccustomed to the use of this gesture. Judith's face is turned slightly toward the wall. She glows from the light emanating there. Her eyes are full of tears. And my hand—committed somewhat independently now to this attempt to redeem the gesture of her father on her last night in his house, to give the gesture the sincerity she so desires—my hand pats away furiously. I am desperate to stop her tears.

"Can you help me to do your will? To sleep?" she asks.

I bring my patting hand to a stop. She and I are both relieved. I lift my hand and her eyes are still lambent with tears and I pass my hand before her and her face disappears and my hand moves on and her face reappears and her eyes are closed and she is asleep until I call her forth again. I am content. She sleeps.

I rise and I make my way down the corridor, a faint snoring or rustling of limbs coming from this cubicle and that. They all are sleeping, my guests, my children, and I believe that they are happy, for this moment at least. They are safe. But then I think of their dreams and I think of Citrus's dream of the man named Jesus and of the nails hammered through his hands and feet and I grow afraid. Is this the role that Citrus would have me play? The stories this species tells itself over and over, through generations, all seem to have certain endings that are inevitable. My fingers grow stiff again in fear. The sounds to the left and to the right, coming from the darkness where these creatures sleep, suddenly drive me forward faster, faster, I am gliding fast, away from the sleepers lest they awaken and see me as Citrus does.

But now there is a turning to the corridor and another and I am before our own living space—mine and my wife Edna Bradshaw's—and I move through the yielding door and Edna is there. She is sitting on our genuine Early American Reproduction Couch with Comfy Built-In Recliner that we brought up from her trailer after our marriage. Eddie the yellow cat is purring loudly in her lap and she has characteristically left the recliner end for me to sit in. She has declared several times that she loves her one true man sitting in a recliner, especially a recliner that she picked out even before she met that man. It was Fate that brought us together. And the recliner is a sign of that.

"Hello, darling, I am home," I say.

"Hello, darling, did you have a hard day?" Edna says.

"I am still having my day," I say, though I know this exchange is supposed to proceed less literally.

"I'm still trying to adjust to that, Desi honey. Are we doing more breakfasts? It's getting on into the afternoon, isn't it? Though I never really know up here."

"Perhaps we will postpone breakfasts for a while," I say.

"Course, it's always breakfast time for our guests, isn't it? Seeing as they're always just waking up after a long sleep?"

"You are making a happy home for me and for our guests," I say. "I rely on your judgment."

This pleases my wife Edna Bradshaw and she beams me a sweet smile and strokes the yellow cat Eddie with increased vigor and she nods her head toward the recliner and waits for me to sit down.

I do. This is a difficult matter for me, but one that I am willing to take on for the sake of my wife Edna Bradshaw. The Comfy Adjustable Headrest thrusts my head forward with extreme Discomfy, from either of its two adjustable positions, and the Doctor Designed Lumbar Control buckles me outward in the middle, perhaps to give the anonymous doctor better access for abdominal surgery, and I pause in this process and Edna says, as she is always quick to do, "Go ahead. Stretch out and relax." And I do what she is convinced—beyond the powers of her observation to contradict—gives me pleasure. And since she is my loving wife, my presumed pleasure clearly gives her pleasure, so I reach down and throw the handle and my torso flies back and my feet fly up and I am Reclining in Total Comfort, or so is the public assertion of those who make and sell and appreciate this machine. But I am far from that promised state. Far. Though I am now reclining, my head remains slung forward, running a hot flame down the back of my neck, and my midsection remains bulged, though now upward, inducing tendrils of pain to snake off my spine so that I find myself wishing for the doctor to get on with the surgery. And my vision is filled with my sixteen toes arrayed in rigid response to the severity of my discomfort.

"There now," Edna says. "Isn't that nice?"

I wish for that to be a true question instead of a joyful declaration. But it is not. She believes unquestioningly in the benefits of this place she has made for me. "Yes," I say, understanding that I suffer this for her.

And she falls silent. I turn my head to look at her as best I can from this position. She is sideways, in profile, partly blocked by the curve of the headrest. But still I can sense a movement of regret in her. I think of the knowing nod she gave me when I saw her last. "Something is on your mind," I say.

Edna replies at once. "For a moment there earlier, with that girl, with me cooking for her and you taking care of her like you do, it was almost like we were her mama and daddy. You know?"

I look at my tentacle-like toes, fixed, from an increasingly complex discomfort, in the middle of the air. I think of my wife Edna Bradshaw's toes.

"Isn't that a sweet thought?" she declares.

Her toes are much shorter than my own.

"You are an excellent mother figure," I say. And there are noticeably fewer of them, her toes.

"I've always wanted that," she says, sitting with both feet flat on the floor, primly so, her feet hidden in her beflowered house slippers, and though her toes are not visible to me, I know that the hard tips of them are red, as red as certain giant stars, made so by her own hand.

"Do I disappoint you?" I ask and this is a real question, for though I am charmed by her toes, they are dramatically different from my own. Not that toes are involved in reproduction on my planet. I am asking a direct question now of my wife but I am thinking in indirections. Her body and mine are different in regrettable ways. We certainly have fundamentally correct parts for each other, mechanically speaking. I am, happily, her spaceman lover as well as her husband. But there are deoxyribonucleic differences.

"No, my dear darling spaceman, you have never disappointed me," she says and I am glad that I hear this not as a further question but as a clear declaration. She even shifts in my direction to emphasize her words and she does this abruptly and single-mindedly enough that Eddie the yellow cat cries out his own sort of words, words that to my untutored ear sound like both un-equivocal declaration and indignant question. "No," Edna says again and I hope that she will not say it a third time and bring the doubt of too much protest into my mind, but she slides farther toward me, Eddie shooting off her lap, her hand fluttering in the space between us, and she says, "I didn't mean that at all."

I say, "I wish for you to have everything in life that you desire."

"Desi honey, I'd given up on being a mama years ago, except maybe to Eddie. Where has he gone now, my little rascal?" She looks around distractedly. Her words notwithstanding, I feel a sadness in her that is unresolved.

"See?" she says, lunging forward, entirely disappearing from my sight. I struggle to rise up a bit from the recliner, but the machine seems mysteriously to create its own gravitational field, for I make little progress in spite of significant effort.

"No," I say, "I do not see."

Edna's voice floats up to me, muffled, from somewhere below, and I realize that she has her head under the couch, look-ing for Eddie in one of his favorite retreats. "I'm a neglectful mama anyway," she says.

"Not at all," I say and I thrash furiously at the black-hole suck of the recliner and still I rise up only enough to free my back from the lump of the lumbar support and I grope now for the handle and throw it and the chair propels me violently forward and I fight the inertia that feels as if it will fling me across the room and my feet slam to the floor and I am a young spaceman cadet once again having just failed my landing test. I quiver for a moment and I turn to Edna. She is planted on the floor on her hands and knees, no longer looking under the couch. She is simply poised there, her head up, thoughtful, her mouth drawn down. "You are not neglect-ful," I say. "You have even learned from him how to stand."

She considers this, observing her own quadrupedal stance. Then she looks at me and says a word that I cannot record. It is a word I am convinced I have heard Eddie the yellow cat speak. A word that is all vowels and understandable, surely, only in its com-plex inflection. When Edna says this word, I think that Eddie's language might, in fact, be even closer to the basic expressiveness of my own species than Edna's language. It is a kind of music. "My wife Edna Bradshaw," I say. "You surprise me. Can you teach me to speak with Eddie the yellow cat?"

"Silly," she says. "I just made that up. I am Edna the slightly flushed but basically white cat."

And at this she moves—with quite surprising grace, given her cat's stance—to the foot of the recliner and she bites me on the ankle.

9 There are three things about this planet which are too wonderful for me. Make that four things. The way of dreams in the mind; the way of tears in the eyes; the way of words in the mouth; and the way of my wife Edna Bradshaw when she acts like a cat and love-nibbles me into her arms.

Ah. Though this is but a quasi-word I feel it appropriate, and say it once more. Ah. Because there are more than four things, as a matter of fact. There are many things about this world that are too wonderful for me to comprehend, several of which Edna Bradshaw and I partook of after she had bitten me on the ankle and extracted me from the recliner. And enough said about that, as they end touchy conversations around the place where my wife Edna Bradshaw once worked, Mary Lou's Southern Belle Beauty Nook, in Bovary, Alabama. Except to say that when I am reminded—even in a pleasurable way—of the mysteries of the planet they call Earth, floppy fingers can turn to flinty fingers in an instant. I have very little time left before I must reveal myself to this world. So little that I am afraid at this moment to calculate it precisely. And so I have left my wife Edna Bradshaw sleeping heavily in our bed, draped gently in the sheet by my own stiffening hands, and I have gone out of our private space, filled with dread. I am happy, however, that I did not show this feeling to my wife. Before she turned over and fell instantly and of her own accord asleep, she whispered, "Oh you spaceman," and she made a sound like the purring of Eddie the cat.

I sit now before the console and I think again of those who are dead. I met Herbert Jenkins in the air. It was during a period of great strife down below, in the year locally designated as 1968, but our selection algorithm found him on an uncharacteristically quiet night near the end of that year in a diner in the city of Chicago. I was not working our vessel alone at the time. But I was already a senior examiner and I did work the watch alone, observing the chosen subject for a while, remotely, engaging in the final, intuitive phase of the decision before acquisition. The diner was small and the hour was late. The man I saw on the screen was part of the primary species group superficially distinguished by a darker skin coloration, though I had already learned that in the minds of some in the world below, the distinction was not superficial, which was an attitude that greatly contributed to the strife of that time. He was alone. I close my eyes, trying to bring back these images that are no longer on record. Only his voice is in my machine. But I want to see him in his own world once more.

He was alone, my old Herbert Jenkins. He had food before him. Yes. I thank my wife Edna Bradshaw for making possible the recall of that fact. More than simply food. He had breakfast before him. He had sausage and eggs and a biscuit and home fries. In my mind I pull back out the window of the diner and I see in neon: BREAKFAST SERVED 24 HOURS. It is cold out here, I realize. There is a frosty haze around a streetlamp. There is dirty snow mounded against the diner's outer wall. A siren sounds in the distance and a dog barks. Herbert Jenkins comes out now. Time has lurched forward in my head. He has finished his breakfast. His coat is too thin. He pulls up his collar and he puffs a plume of his breath into the dark. On that night thirty-two years ago it was time to encounter this man, and I moved my hand to the panel to bring him up to the spaceship, and now I move my hand to hear his voice again, and I find my fingers stiff before me. Lately this has been happening with alarming frequency, these spasms of fear. In my memory I have also paused. And both of me watch Herbert Jenkins hunch his shoulders against the cold and turn to walk away. And this is why I am afraid: I am Herbert Jenkins. *Yessir, I did too have a suit just like yours. Lord have mercy. I feel like a fool thinking back on it. Not that you should. I don't mean it like that. You look fine for a space alien. But I was the oldest zoot-suiter on the South Side of Chicago in and about 1942. Fit me just pretty much like it fits you there. But when I was togged to the bricks in bluff cuffs, I could jump with my angel cake till it was brightin'. And that's the Bible.*

Now listen to me there. I haven't thought of those words for twenty some-odd years. Not to mention let them pass out of my mouth. Not even sure I could tell you what they all mean right now, exactly. But my zoot suit was the color of a singing canary and I was big inside that thing, real big, and all those words I said was like singing. I was forty-four years old at that time. My one child, my daughter Carolyn, was living with her husband by then in Milwaukee and my wife, Sadie, bless her heart, which was big as all of Lake Michigan, she went along with my second adolescence just fine. I miss her bad now, I can tell you. I was hoping when you took me up that I just had died and I was about to see her again.

Some people think the zoots was a Mexican thing. But our man Cab Calloway was the first to billboard himself like that, make his shoulders wide and his drape long and you could see that he was master of something, bigger than anybody would expect him to be. Not that I'm saying the Mexicans couldn't be like that, too. They went through the troubles like we did, I expect. And they paid for their threads with blood out in Los Angeles. In '43, I think it was. There was an actual zoot suit riot, with the police and the soldiers and the sailors out there hunting down the cats with the reet pleats and beating them to death for being who they are.

Doesn't take much, does it, for the bad guys to go putting a world of hurt on you. These things going on in Chicago today and Detroit and all around. In my own street. People forget it's happened before in this town. I come here with my daddy and my mammy from Mississippi before the first war and I was just a kid. Missed that war, too. I was too young. Like I was too old for the second one. Not that it was so easy to be able to fight for your country if you was a Negro, but I would've tried. Still, let's see, what was I? I was nineteen when President Wilson finally had to start sending us over. I guess I could've died in France or somewhere at nineteen. But like I say, it was a known fact that they didn't want Negro kids in the Army. We wasn't worthy of dying for a country.

What we could die for was a water fountain or a seat on a bus or some damn miserable little thing like that. Or a place to swim. See, there was a riot—just like this one—back right after the first war. It was a real hot summer, July or August, and it must have been about 1919. A Negro boy was out swimming in the lake and somehow he got in a current or something or he got turned around. But anyways he show up just off the shore at the Twenty-ninth Street beach and that was forbidden. People think it was just the South that have a white this and a colored that, but we couldn't go nowhere near the Twenty-ninth Street beach at that time. That was before the whole South Side from Twenty-sixth to Fifty-first and from the lake to the Rock Island tracks had gone and turn into Bronzeville. We was already living pretty thick over near the railroad but there was still a bunch of German Jews and Irish Catholics living in the area, especially along Douglas and Grand Boulevard and they let us clean their houses but we couldn't mess up the water off their shores. So some of those boys saw this Negro swimming out there and they threw stones against him till he went down and drowned. Just for being in the water.

Lookit. There's this thing that happens right here in the center of my chest when I say that. Right now. That's interesting to me. I get to thrashing around in there. It's enough that I might could do something real angry if I was a young man still, or even a forty-four-year-old man, and if I let myself dwell on what they did to Reverend King and what they did to Muhammad Ali and what they doing to all our Negro boys in this war in Vietnam. It's only too easy now for a Negro to die in a war. And nobody kids himself it's to save our country or save the world or nothing like that. So let the Negroes die in Vietnam, they be thinking. Do us all some good.

I don't know why I didn't go and get into fights and burn some things down when I was twenty-one years old and we had a week or more of fighting in the streets over that boy being stoned to death in Lake Michigan. Guess it was 'cause I only just did started out at the Stockyards and I was glad to have a job, even for fifteen dollars a week, and even if it was just as a driver at that time, wading around ankle-deep in pig shit herding those animals from train car to holding pen and from holding pen to killing room.

Even going to work, though, I had my chances to do something about how I felt. There was plenty of Irish living west of the Rock Island tracks, in between us and the Yards, in a place they called Canaryville. I think Mayor Daley lives there right now. And I remember we had to go through there to get to work, through that Irish neighborhood, and it was real rough, especially during that week or two in 1919. We took some tough words and we took some spit and all like that. But I just turned the other cheek, so to speak. No matter how angry I was inside.

I guess I feel a little ashamed of that now. I had plenty of cause to act on this thrash-around feeling in the center of me back then. I was a young man. I could've picked up a rock and throwed it. Or done something. And I can be thinking about white folks like they think about us. Whitey this. Whitey that. Ain't no good Whitey but a dead Whitey. But lookit here. I figure that'd be a way for those white people who be racists, all the dumb shits with the bed sheets on or the spit flying out of *their filthy mouths, it'd be a way for them to get the Negro real good once and for all. You know how that is? By turning us into them, that's how. Make us think like they do. Make us see a color, no matter what it is, even if it's white, and we think we know that person because of it. If we do the Whitey this and the Whitey that, then we're being just like them boys in the sheets. That'd give them a good laugh, wouldn't it. See, I got to go back now and say that in the time they killed that Negro boy who was just swimming out in the lake, it was only some particular Irish Catholics and German Jews who done it. I know there be plenty of good folks among them, just like we want them to know that we got plenty of good folks among us.*

Still you get mad. You know? You still got to deal with that feeling in your chest. That's probably partly why I was wearing a zoot suit when I was forty-four years old. I got robbed of something long before that. Like that boy in the lake. He was maybe twelve, thirteen years old and there was nothing more for him in this life. He got robbed of his childhood, is what. Well, that's what happened to me, too. What happened to most of us. You don't live like we all lived in those times from the cradle on up and ever get to wear the bright colors and the big shoulders and the floppy pants of childhood. That's what they took from us and what I tried to get back dressing up like you there, Mr. Space Alien. I'm ready to believe there be some real good folks among you Space People, too. I hope you had a nice childhood. I sure wonder what it would've been like. But I want to shake your hand because I am not a prejudiced man. I won't never let that happen to me. Man, you've got a lot of fingers. But that's hep, Jackson. Meeting you's money from home.

This voice vanishes now into the darkness. I look at my strikingly befingered hand and I think of slapping the skin with Herbert Jenkins and I am glad to have thought of him, to have listened to him at this moment. I realize that part of my present terror, facing my assignment, comes from a sense of those below who will look upon my body and be ravished by its differences from their own and see in me only their fears which they will turn to prejudice and then to hatred and then to rage and then to murder. Have things changed so much down there in the subsequent thirty-two revolutions about this frankly mediocre star? Dear Herbert Jenkins. I wish I could move my hand and bring back your body from that great darkness that puzzles us together, your species and mine. I wish I could hear new words from you. And that is the Bible.

10

The cowardice that came upon me in the corridor outside my guests' sleeping quarters lingers in me now. I do not wish to seek any new voices. I miss my dear Herbert Jenkins, it is true. But it is also true that he is known to me and he is gone from me and that is an attraction to a coward. It is easier to give one's devotion to the dead than to the living.

I rise. I make myself move out the door and back to the place where they lie dreaming. I am alone. I am flesh and blood, and though my blood is the color of Presbyterian Punch, it flows just as easily and disastrously as the blood of those who have been assaulted by prejudice and fear on this planet.

I am amidst the snoring and sighing and rustling now. Perhaps from respect for Herbert Jenkins I am moved to approach the man called Hudson.

"Hudson Smith, Esquire, attorney at law," he elaborates in his half-sleep as I lead him down the corridor and into the place where our voices can join.

He sits. He wakes further. He looks at me.

"I'd advise you people to stay away from this planet," he says, though his voice is gentle, almost sad.

I say, "There are some on my home planet who share that opinion."

"They're right," he says. "Though maybe it'd be just the thing to finally fix race relations down there. The Irish and the English and the Poles and the Italians and so forth, they all finally stopped fighting each other in America when they agreed on the black folks to unify their hate. Maybe a bunch of folks who look like you would unify whites and blacks just the same way. We can all hate the gray bug-eyes together."

This is not what I want to hear. But it is necessary, I tell myself. It is better to understand what awaits me.

A change comes over Hudson. He shifts in his chair, leans forward, his hand comes out toward me, lingering in the air between us. "I'm sorry," he says. "I get caught up in my own fight and here I sit saying ugly things about you right to your face. My daddy'd whup me up side of my head for that and I'd deserve it."

I nod and I suppose I should engage this self-reflecting male from this parallel species in a dialogue. But I am weary. And I wish to hear his inner self. So I wave my hand and I let go of Desi, I let go of my own inner voice. I am Hudson Smith. *My father. I think of my father all the time. He believed in the Melting Pot. Nobody talks that shit anymore. The goddamn American dream. But God bless him, my father, he wouldn't let any of us be anything but excellent and it was because of that big motherfucking Pot he could see in his head, that thing he thought this country was. You could go into the Pot as a beer-truck driver in Alexandria, Louisiana, which is what he was, and through your children, you could come out a Harvard lawyer, which is what became of his youngest son that he named after a river he never saw. That was me. And he also came out a pediatrician in Cleveland, a University of Chicago English professor, a Proctor and Gamble product manager, and so forth. We were eight of us—my father's little black babies—which is what he still called us when he could get us all together. Not that that was very often, after we did what he told us to do and became excellent and scattered all over the country. When we did get together, for a wedding or once in a while for Christmas, and he had his captive audience*

at the dinner table, before we could eat he'd start orating to his grown-
up babies on the virtues of this Land of the Free where anything is possible, this being the very same table we grew up at and heard him question
each one of us about our day, every day, and press us to do better, to be
excellent all the time because we were worthy of excellence. We were
worthy. And my mother was the same way. You could watch her cut a
goddamn carrot into a pot and you'd know she was determined to do it
better than anybody who ever cut a carrot before.

　　And if Wilhelmina and I had gone on and had a kid before she
decided to grab the Lexus and God knows what else she's going to get
before this is over—no matter how good a lawyer my father's youngest
son is—if we'd had our own little African-American, culturally re-rooted,
powerfully independent baby—how could I say the things to him that
had done so much good to me? If I tried to say my own father's words to
him, I'm afraid they'd sound like lies. They'd sound like the bullshit of
White America, trying to take away the dignity of somebody who was
different from them. Get rid of your blackness. Melt down here and make
it tan. Keep melting and we might even recognize you. Eggshell white.

　　We still crave that recognition. So many of us do. And it creates
powerful heroes for us. Heroes as in archetypal heroes, bigger than life
and carrying around in their bodies a bit of all of us, and they're also
carrying some real old baggage with them. Baggage full of feelings. Feelings that got melted into everyfuckingbody a long time ago. Take OJ, for
instance.

　　Now that surely is a creature from the Melting Pot. O. J. Simpson
come up out of there and he was a football hero and he was a movie star
and he was running through airports pimping Hertz cars and he had
this smooth off-white charm and he was good to every kid he saw and he
had a gorgeous white wife so if you were white, you knew he didn't hate
you for it, and if you were black, you knew that here was a black man
that whites not only would share a water fountain with, they'd go to bed

*with and have his kids—and if with him, then with us—and we all loved
him, we all got melted down together in our love for this American hero.*

*So when he murdered that wife—and yo, wake up, I'm a lawyer
and I look at the evidence, and if I'm the Man, if I'm Johnny on-the-spot
Cochran, if I'm Johnny I-make-a-rhyme-and-he-don't-do-time Cochran,
I do the same defense he does because of course there's racists in the LA
Police, but anybody whose business it is to look at evidence and look at
human nature is going to know in his bones OJ is guilty—I'm no traitor
to my race to say he murdered her—so when O. J. Simpson murdered
his wife, how'd we get to fooling ourselves about the truth, those of us of
color, those of us who have—thank God—come around at the end of
the twentieth century to finally telling the truth, generally, about where
we are and what we are and what it is that we've been having to deal
with all these years? Why are we going against our smart natural selves
and making this man out to be innocent?*

*Well, it's that archetypal thing, is why. Because OJ is a tragic hero,
is why. He's a good man. He's a bigger-than-life man. He's a man who
carries with him the vested identity of a whole people. But he's got a flaw.
He's jealous. Like all of us. But since everything else about him is big,
so's this flaw. And once—just once—he's in a circumstance that the
universe has done up for him and his flaw makes him do something terrible. And the universe is ready to punish him big time. But he's not just
him, he's you. He's your own human capacity for doing a bad thing under
a certain circumstance. And it scares the shit out of you. And so you make
it untrue. You turn it all into a mistake. Better, you make it the work of
the devil, a deception and a lie of the sort you've been hearing all your
life directed at you. If you took Oedipus Rex, who kills his own father in
a similar hot-blooded thing and he marries his mother, and you set down
twelve Greeks, who see their very selves in Oedipus, and you say—okay,
here's the end of the tragedy, but the writer's going to defer to you. You
make the ending. Should he pluck out his eyes and die? If it's up to them,*

they're going to say, Shit no. It's all a mistake. He's innocent. Which is what a bunch of our people did. Those twelve on the jury and millions more, as well. Millions and millions.

And I can understand that. OJ will go on and never kill again and he'll be a warm and loving father to his kids, and I can't help but think of my own father. He loved OJ. Of course he did. OJ was what my father knew his kids could become. You go out and be excellent. You're worthy of that. And people will come to love you. Black people and white people and brown people and yellow people and red people. You stop along the way and be nice to the folks who love you. Sign those autographs. Kiss those women. Bring us together in the stands, all of America, to cheer what a boy can do who's got a lot to overcome but he did it. This is the land of opportunity.

And my father died before that dark and star-crossed night in June of 1994 in Los Angeles. But I know he would have continued to believe in OJ like so many others. And he never would have spoken of it to me, since he knew who I was and how I saw things, and he loved me for it, though he stopped being able to agree with me about much of anything. We would've just never spoken of it, like for years we never spoke anymore of the Melting Pot, though he did continue to lecture me now and then, a few sentences at a time, on the telephone.

And I will never be able to tell him I'm sorry. But I am. I'm sorry, Daddy, for thinking you were, for all your life, a poor deceived old Negro, but I do think that, and I don't like that in me, and I know I'd never be what I am today, free to think these thoughts, free to be excellent, if it wasn't for you believing in those lies in the first place. That irony is not lost on me. And I'm grateful to you, Daddy. I'm grateful and sorry as shit.

I keep my Hudson Smith in his dream state as I lead him back to his bed. It strikes me that after observing his spiritedness at the Welcome-to-the-Spaceship party, I had hoped Hudson's voice

would be, even issuing from his deep and secret place, a voice of
unalloyed self-confidence, exempt from the tyranny of yearning.
But I was wrong.

I guide Hudson into his cubicle and he readily lies down and
for the sake of his lost father I tuck him in, pressing the covers up
under his chin, and his head lolls away and I think that he will
sleep. Then suddenly his hand is on my arm. I gasp.

But he is a gentle man, I have come to realize. He holds my
arm with something like tenderness and he looks up at me, his
eyelids drooping toward sleep, and he says, "Thank you."

I pat his hand and it lets go of me and retreats under the covers and he is asleep. I stand and look at him for a moment. I try to
think of the boldest, most confident voice in our memory banks.

I rush back to our great panel of babble. Something in here
must have meaning for me. Somewhere there must be a resolu-
tion. The categories before me are meaningless: age, gender, race.
The voices all elude their categories. And they all alarm me.

Here. A voice I remember as bold. *Ecdysiast. Call me an ecdysiast
and nothing else or I'll sock you in the chops.* Her voice is spilling into
the room on its own, even before I can make my own voice one with
hers. But that is not strictly true. For she is dead and she is gone and
it is my hand that passes over this panel, that lets her captured sounds
return. She has no independent will anymore. But I ignore this hard
fact for the moment. Instead, I whisper to her, aloud, as if she is in
the room, "Wait for me, Scarlet." *I don't let nobody ever call me a strip-
per. I don't care if that comes across as hoity-toity. I am Scarlet. Like
my name. I've got certain principles and if the pock-faced gropy-handed
tiny-dicked club owners don't like it then they can lump it. It's Scarlet
Moscowitz. Not Scarlet LaRue. Not Scarlet Belle. Not Scarlet O'Dare.
Not anything made up at all. Though the Scarlet part is. That's true
enough. But that's okay. That's a given name anyway and I got as much*

right to give it as anybody else. More right. But I'm Moscowitz. That's it. That's from my daddy and from his daddy before him and nobody's gonna fuck with it. And if I choose to take off my clothes before a room full of whoever wants to see it—even if they're most of them drunks and no-goods—then you have to understand what it is exactly that I'm doing. I'm not stripping. I'm molting. That's what ecdysiast means. You can look it up. And now, presenting for your extreme pleasure for one night only, the beautiful ecdysiastical spectacle of Scarlet Moscowitz. And I am dressed in a shimmering red dress up to my throat and down to my toes and it's the most beautiful dress you've ever seen, twenty thousand scarlet spangles—my given name cried out loud by a great crowd twenty thousand strong all hollering at once. But even so, this isn't really me. Not the final me. If I just stayed like this, in this beautiful dress, there'd be trouble. Those men out there would tear the place apart with rage and disappointment. Because the dress of twenty thousand red spangles is like the caterpillar skin. It's just a stage. The real me is what they want. And that's what I give them. I molt. The old skin, the lesser skin, it just falls away and there I am, the real me, and they're happy, they're whooping in pleasure. As beautiful as that dress was, it isn't as beautiful as this. I'm the butterfly now. I stand before them in my naked flesh, Miss Scarlet Moscowitz, and they might be drunks and they might be no-goods but they can see that I'm beautiful.

And I wipe her voice away. Because I hear at last what I'd never heard in this self-confident voice before. When Scarlet spoke to me, a young spaceman newly arrived above this world, and she was a woman old beyond her years and sick nearly to death, she said no more about her father than to explain why she kept her family name. But I realize now that on Burlesque stages across America, from the Day That Will Live in Infamy to the Day of Sputnik, my Scarlet Moscowitz stood naked, time and time again, before her father. Her drunken no-good father who never saw for a moment the beauty of his daughter who loved him, loved him faith-fully, and who held his name close to her and who yearned for him to see her as these others saw her. As whoopingly beautiful.

Dance for *me*, Scarlet. Dance for your spaceman father. I will be all the things for you that he was not. I can look upon your body—ample as it is, concisely fingered and toed as it is—and I know I will see it as beautiful.

But Scarlet's body is dust and bones now.

This was not the voice I needed to hear.

I crack my knuckles. But this time the gesture does not soothe me. It only thickens my sadness. Whiplash Willie is dead, too, of course. Willie with his own yearnings, his own keenly felt failures. I myself yearn for a Life from this planet to sit before me and speak its inner words and be, if not happy, then at least content, and if not content, then at least drably unconsidered and bland. One might expect such lives in abundance down there, growing like wheat. But I have found not even one. Not in all the days and nights and days and nights that have passed below me since I first came here. Not one. Not one, even in all these voices that awaited me in our machinery, collected by others long before I arrived. Not one. And I feel, even now, even for the ones who are dead, I feel. What? I feel what? I feel.

That bit of rhetorical irresolution is the fullest expression I am capable of. Like another trill of words that moves in me at certain moments: I am. I am. I feel. I wish to say to each life that sits before me and has just finished speaking, "Arise, and be not afraid."

I arise now, and I am sore afraid. I feel. I am.

No one has spoken to me yet of *LUCK*, of that grand golden purpose of the late-night bus trip from the Great State of Texas to the State of Louisiana where they Let the Good Times Roll. But, of course, I have only spoken to three of the travelers so far, and one of those was the driver of the bus. I should put aside the voices from the past and listen anew. I desperately need new words, new lives spoken through my voice. There is so much I still do not understand, and I am keenly aware of the shortness of time. Once again I do not stop to calculate exactly how much. But I know to fear that I will not even have enough time to speak with everyone now sleeping on my ship. I should speak to another of my visitors right now.

But I know that first I will do something rash. I have little hope of encountering, among the travelers on the bus, the sort of life I presently wish to study. It is time to spend a few hours on the planet surface. When the night returns to the place beneath my ship, I will go down, personally, in my very body. I will go with great caution, disguised in the trench coat and wide-brimmed felt hat I wore when I first met Edna Bradshaw in the nearly deserted parking lot of the all-night Wal-Mart Supercenter in Bovary, Alabama. My five-hour mission will be to seek out a kind of life new to my studies, a life full of bland contentedness. A life without yearning.

And though I should gather another voice or two from my present visitors before I go, instead, I return to find my wife Edna Bradshaw still sleeping on our bed. And I lie down beside her and I seek out my own sleep, where dreams never intrude and the Hills Are Alive with the Sound of Music, except there are no hills, either, not even the ups and downs of a landscape. Just music.

11

And I wake. I sense it is time for my mission. Edna, I am happy to see, is still beside me, though she stirs now. I move my hand across her and she grows quiet once more. I do not wish for her to wake while I am gone and be alarmed at my absence. I lean to her and touch my fingertips to her face and I hope that she can see me in her dreams, that she can hear my heartbeat there.

I slip away quietly to my preparation room and I open the storage space and I resolve to take extra precautions. I will have layers of disguise: Before the trench coat and felt hat, I become togged to the bricks in bluff cuffs, and I choose the tie that I wore on my first date with my angel cake Edna Bradshaw, a red one with dozens of Tabasco bottles floating on it. She seemed to love that tie. I even put on my size-twenty Converse Chuck Taylor All Star sneakers. Encapsulating footwear is unknown on my planet, and I am still not used to the concept, but I will take no chances on this night. I don my trench coat and cinch the belt, though not too revealingly tight because of what Edna refers to as my Scarlett O'Hara waist—which I understand to refer to its minimal girth—my waist was the first clue to give me away as a spaceman on the night I met her—and I put on my hat and pull the wide brim down low.

It is night. I am ready. I squeak down the corridor in my Chuck Taylors, which are the color, I am pleased to note, of Herbert Jenkins's bluff cuffs, that is to say, the color of a singing canary.

My zoot suit, however, is conservative in color, gray with pinstripes. My trench coat is black, as is my hat. I am a Dude.

And the Dude is behind the wheel of his honker. So to speak. I have no wheel and I have no horn, but I sit in my shuttle ship and I am ready to spin off into the world below and I flex at my fingers, which are turning me into a coward. But to be honest, it is the coward in me that is producing this frequent stiffening in my fingers, not the other way around. In all the Earth years I have been watching this planet, I have actually and personally been to its surface perhaps six or eight times and I have never been in peril. The last time I even came to carry away the woman who fell in love with me the time before. But the time after this one will be so momentous that I am full of anxiety now. And there are always risks, of course. Outside of my spaceship I still have the power to induce sleep and forgetfulness, but only within a very limited physical area. There are many circumstances, in an alien terrain, over which I would have no control whatsoever.

But I put these thoughts from my mind and I launch forth and I rush toward the lights below, veering now to the dark edges of the city, mindful of the searching green strobes from the casino boats. I am being excessively cautious. Though my craft is shrouded, pilot errors can, of course, occur, especially in the transition between modes of propulsion, thus giving an observer below a glimpse of what they call a UFO. But this is a rare phenomenon and I am alert tonight. So I let myself move over the thickenings of trees with streets between and dwellings set side by side by side by side. If the placid lives I seek exist, surely they will be along these quiet streets. I move quickly back and forth and I look for a place to land my craft. Open, preferably dim, with no one apt to walk unsuspecting into an invisible thing. I grow bold. I move over a great ship taking on rice in the orange wash of sodium vapor

lamps and I rush along the edge of the lake. The houses here are
large and full of the fruits of capitalism and yet I feel a great striving emanating from them and I cut inland and ahead I see what I
think for a moment is a Wal-Mart and I grow nostalgic, thinking
of the night in Bovary, Alabama, when Edna called out to me as I
stood alone and separate, very late into the time of daily darkness,
and there were only four scattered vehicles about and no living
creatures at all, not until my future wife came out of her shopper's
paradise and spotted me from afar and then called out in sympathetic concern over what, I later realized, she presumed was my
misplaced vehicle. "Are you lost?" she said. I am.

And now I see that the place before me is not a Wal-Mart
after all. I swoop around it, and the place proclaims itself KROGER
FAMILY CENTER OPEN 24 HOURS DRUGS FOOD and next to
it, across a street, is a vast open space of fissured concrete, not
ideally dim, but clearly abandoned, the structure that was once
there reduced to a faint outline of its foundation. I swoop and return. There are railroad tracks running along a street past the front
of Kroger, past this open space, and then at an angle across that
same street and down a median and heading into the night in the
direction of the ship at the lake. I swoop, slowing, and there is a
sign at the edge of the open space, dark and fractured: ROLLER
RINK.

I land. I wait. It is late. It is dim here in the center of Roller
Rink. I wonder what Roller Rink was. I wonder why such a thing
has escaped my notice over the years. Perhaps for the same reason
that it has now been reduced to an empty swath of concrete and a
crumbling sign. Something went terribly wrong. Once Roller Rink
was as proud an edifice of the planet Earth as Kroger or Wal-Mart,
but those of this world turned against it and it crumbled into
emptiness.

My mind is overheating. I even imagine the people of Lake Charles, Louisiana, storming Roller Rink with pitchforks and burning torches crying for its death, tearing it apart with their hands. But I know how *words* always strive to be something other than they are, to gather around the thing they have their eyes on and run at it from the shadows, from unexpected directions, I know this about the *words* on this planet and so I know, in fact, I am not pondering the past fate of Roller Rink but the imminent fate—*very* imminent, I am afraid—of the spaceman known as DESI who has been ordered to expose his actual physical self in a grand and irrefutable and unambiguous way to all the people of this world and to share a fundamental truth of the universe. Come Quick. *It's Alive!*

Lookit, I say to myself. I could have sat and dreaded the future back on the home spacecraft without the unpleasantness of wearing sneakers. If I am going to make this visit, I should Just Do It. The street beyond the train track is empty. The street between Roller Rink and Kroger is empty. The Kroger parking lot has only a scattered few cars and no creature is visible. So I step from my craft.

The air is quite mild and it smells faintly of wood fire. A dog barks in the distance. The sky to the west is tinted orange from oil refineries, and there, cutting above the distant rim of trees and then sliding silently off, is the thread of green light from the casinos. But my way lies into the quiet streets of the neighborhood. I move through the vanished Roller Rink, resolving to ask my wife Edna Bradshaw about this place, and I stop at the street and look over at the Kroger parking lot.

I never did actually enter Wal-Mart that night in Bovary, Alabama. Our machines have given us views, of course, inside all of the various edifices on this planet, but there is something that cannot be reproduced through any technology. On this planet, one has to stand in a place, in one's own body, to understand its influence on the lives here. That is one reason why I am taking these risks right now. There is an ethos to every spot. I look around. I have moved perhaps fifty paces from my craft, which, I am happy to observe, is invisible in the Roller Rink space. But things are quite different, even just over here. For instance, I can no longer smell burning wood. Instead, there is a smell of trees. Fir trees. They are piled off the street curb to my right. A dozen small, scrawny trees, intended, I know—how spotty and minute is my understanding of this place—intended to be placed in the home at this time of the year and decorated with lights to celebrate the birth of the man for whom Citrus mistook me on the spaceship earlier, a celebration whose primary day has recently passed. I hesitate here with the dead trees, which were apparently too thin to have been worth purchasing—I presume in a sales operation across the street at this Kroger Family Center, in spite of its avowal simply to provide DRUGS and FOOD, or perhaps in the space of this departed Roller Rink— whichever, the trees would be trucked in and piled up and sold and then the excess dumped, as with this dozen trees—I am conscious of the ways of commerce on this planet and you do what you can to make a buck and if you can sell ice cubes to Eskimos, you go for it—though why that phrase should leap into me in this context, I have no idea, because though it does have to do with commerce, its application is misplaced in this circumstance, for Kroger's customers would have more use for a holiday tree than an Eskimo would have for ice—but standing here, I sense myself drifting erratically on a thin smoke of nervous words, sounding once again like my wife Edna Bradshaw, and I wish I was with her now, lying beside her on our bed as she sleeps her image-laden sleep.

However, I am not. I am here. And the thought from which I started to drift is this: The place where I stand at this moment is new to me. Perhaps that thought wasn't the exact starting point, but it is close to it. And this is true of the planet Earth: fifty paces away, things are different. Drastically so, if you are alert. And fifty paces more, five paces even, the world will change once again. There is no dog barking now. I hear the mechanical click of the traffic light as the tint on my hands changes from green to amber and then another click as it changes from amber to red. In short, though I can acquire clear images of Kroger from my machines, I do not truly know Kroger, do not know its essence, and so I wish to enter into that place, squeaking across its floor in my Chuck Taylor sneakers. But I am held back by recognizing the inherent risks in doing this, perhaps manageable risks at this hour but perhaps not. The traffic light clicks again and I look up and the large red eye closes and the large green eye opens, and I realize how far from the inherent characteristics of mind of a member of my own species I have been borne. I would say "borne by words" but I can hear how I am sounding on that matter, as well. I have become a whiner. Kvetch. Kvetch. That is all I hear out of me. And surely I am not out of my normal mind simply because of words. Perhaps I should go with the flow. My wife Edna Bradshaw frequently shows evidence of this same syndrome of rambling free association and she is clearly not alarmed by it, indeed seems almost to enjoy it, rolling words out of her head that follow one tiny bright object until it passes another one and then veers off following that one and so on and so on. I look down at my sneakers. Their yellowness, like a singing canary, like Herbert Jenkins's zoot suit—though I never actually saw his zoot suit—the yellowness of my Chuck Taylor All Star sneakers has paled and darkened here on the street at night. But now, Click. The yellow sharpens a bit. From the streetlight again. I look at the light, straight into its amber eye. "Oh shut up your incessant clicking," I say aloud. And it clicks again.

This is not your planet, it says. And it opens its red eye and glares hotly at me. It is the air, causing this wandering. As much as words. It is the smell of smoke, which I am picking up again. And the smell of dead trees. And the dog barking again. No, a different dog, in some other, distant place. I am rushing, inside. It is not the words that are carrying me. The words and I are companions. We are being carried together on this deeper current inside me, which itself comes from the smoke and the trees and the dogs and a thousand other nuances of the night. The click of the street light. The orange glow of the western sky. The rasp of grit beneath my sneakers at the tiniest movement of my feet. The smooth-contoured inertness of the cars in the Kroger lot. And perhaps the words, after all, as well. On my own planet, the primary focus of our lives, moment to moment, is inside our minds, and to touch each other, we leap cleanly across the sensual particularities of our outer world, hardly noticing them at all. But on a planet built with *words,* which are valenced with the same charge as streetlight clicks and dog barks and sneaker rasps, I must deal directly with all these things of the senses lying between my inner world and the inner world of anyone else. I have no choice. And they run deep in me, these sensual things. In ways that both demand and defy the words. Suddenly I find my hands floppy with desire. I think of dear Edna Bradshaw. Edna, come quick. *It's alive!*

I am unsteady now on my feet. I must not think. I step off the curb. I move through the Kroger parking lot, circling to the back, fighting off the impulse to take a chance. I cross the train track. I enter a quiet street, leading directly away from Kroger. It is a street named for a class of bryophytic plants which have a small, leafy, often tufted stem which bears its sex organs at the tip. Do not ask me why it was named after such a thing. Perhaps the place was once covered with *moss.* Perhaps the builder of this street first lay down in a vast blanket of moss, right here, and dreamed of the thing he would build. I move on this street of Moss. Intently now. Trying to hold back the words for a bit, so that I don't stop in any one square of this sidewalk and spend the rest of the night rendering my words around its unique vantage point on the night. I move on, my sneakers scraping and popping, and I press my attention back to my original intent.

I look in the passing windows, ready to go closer, ready to approach an isolated someone, wave my hand before his face, loosen his words, hear him speak of his contentment—in taking out the trash, in thinking about his father, in facing his work, in living his life on this planet. He would speak in a voice I have not yet heard.

A tree lies on its side by the curb, silver threads of tinsel clinging to it, and I look to the house, a porch swing, a shutter sagging slightly away from a broken hinge, the windows dark, no one there. But now there is a movement, even in the dimness of the unlit front room. I slow my step, only vaguely discerning the figure there, a man, I think, moving for a moment in the darkness and then stopping, standing there. The next house drifts into my view and it is bright but I am wondering about the man I have just seen. Only briefly: his tree thrown hastily from the house, him sitting awake in a dark room only to stand and go nowhere. My machines are full of voices no different from his.

I focus, instead, on this bright house before me, the front window outlined in amber bulbs, the tree still standing inside, ablaze with white lights. I see through the front room and through an arch to a table in the dining room and people are there. I stop. A happy family. Contented with their lives. I take a step toward them, onto their lawn, and another step. I am not alone. Something has told me that all along. Perhaps it is the nose, shining as brightly as the streetlight near Kroger. It is Santa Claus, who stands, inanimate, of course, but life-size, beside an azalea bush. What a sense of holiday whimsy resides in this place. How could there be angst and striving and conflict and disconnection in such a family as this? And there they sit, beneath a chandelier—a cheap chandelier, I realize, its bare bulbs poking out of cloudy glass flower blossoms. Good. There is no pretense here. Only harmony and contentment. At least complacent drabness. A woman is in a chair with her back to me, a young woman, I think, given what I know of hairstyles from my wife Edna Bradshaw. Her hair is long and draped straight behind her. She is very thin. Her skin, which I can see on her arm, is pale. I angle a little to the side as I take more steps toward this house. I can hear the murmur of voices. A window is open somewhere, I think. The night, though in the first stages of the winter season on this part of the planet, is very mild. It is the state of Louisiana, after all, Where Winter Comes to Party. Opposite the young woman at the table is another woman, the wife and mother, her hair short and permed, her face haggard, her mouth drawn down. Perhaps given this appearance by the bared bulb light coming from above. She has been preparing this wonderful meal all day long and she is pleasantly weary and the light shows this on her face. She is looking across at her daughter. Next to both of them at the head of the table is a man, the husband and father. He is leaning forward as if listening, but not to these two women. There are others out of my sight, at the opposite end of the table. The murmur I hear is another male voice, the words rushing and tumbling. And then suddenly the husband and father laughs. He leans back in his chair and throws his head back and laughs.

And his wife and his daughter do not move. Not even to glance in his direction. They are as implacable as the Santa Claus standing next to me, shining his cold red light into the darkness. And I know I have misjudged them all.

I back away, out of their yard. This is what I need. I have come here with my own agenda, but I must look at this world the way it is, so that I will know what to do when I soon return.

I hear the distant cry of a train whistle.

This is a sound that my wife Edna Bradshaw has referred to with great wistfulness, a sound that gave her pleasure to hear when she was alone with her yellow cat Eddie in the middle of the night in her trailer at the trailer park out the state highway that connected Bovary, Alabama, with the rest of what she knew to be the world. This was before she and I had met in the parking lot of Wal-Mart. And she was made happy by the thought that there were all those other lives going on in places far away—suggested to her by the sound of a train going somewhere in the night—but she was right there in a place she knew so well. I think that is the reason she turned me down the first time I asked her to fly away with me. She was content.

I straighten and quake with this thought. I plucked Edna Bradshaw from the very sort of life I went seeking on this night.

But no. She was not content. We met, I asked her for a date, I took her out, we fell in love, I was to be transferred, I asked her to marry me, she said no, I went away. But then she was suddenly very unhappy. Bovary, Alabama, no longer gave her pleasure. She heard this sound of a train whistle—and there it is again, coming nearer, but slowly—she heard this sound after I left, and it only made her sad. Made her yearn to follow it. She wanted to fly from what she had always known, a life that no longer satisfied her.

I look toward Kroger and I find that I, too, am yearning.

The bright lights are calling me. I am afraid that the life without yearning, which I sought, does not exist on this world. Perhaps it does not exist at all, anywhere in the universe, so long as creatures have minds and hearts and must move from one moment to the next. For example, I should go now to my undetected shuttle craft and return to my place in the middle of the air. But, in fact, I yearn to understand Kroger, which, I realize, is to yearn to know more about what is to come, for me. It is one thing for me to sneak around in the dark, unobserved, and smugly believe I understand these creatures. It is another thing to walk into that great swath of fluorescent light, which is full of beer and laundry soap and breakfast cereal and conditioning rinse and the ardent seekers of these things, and to say, Look here, you all, you are not the only beings in the universe.

I step across the steel rail and I move into the parking lot and I am full of hope. I know this place teems with the objects that breed in the physical space between these creatures, the objects that beckon and gather and beget *words,* words that have shaped my understanding of things in so many ways. And though I have collected and preserved a number of these objects in a certain dedicated space on my ship, and though they even clutter together there in some profusion, there is an inevitable air of artificiality about my collection, like a case full of insects stuck with pins. I need to be inside Kroger, no matter what the risk. I squeak on quickly across the asphalt, the bright white glow calling me, a cheery WELCOME and a vast yellow Smiley Face over the double automatic doors.

I am suddenly struck by this face, which I have seen through my observation machines in many places. But until this moment I have not seen it for what it truly is, the face of a spaceman. No ears. No hair. Large eyes. No lips but a wide, sweet smile. I am a friendly guy, after all. Perhaps this face has prepared a way for me. This word of welcome is for me, Desi the Friendly Spaceman, making a special appearance at the Family Center, *Have a nice millennium*. I rush toward KROGER.

A figure is standing there, a large figure in a tan uniform, a security guard, I realize, given the lateness of the hour. And I also realize that I am ready to present myself directly to him: Hi, my name is Desi; I'm the spaceman you have been waiting for, whose image floats cheerily over your head even as we speak. And as soon as I think of saying these words, all that I have imagined for myself crumbles at once. I pull my hat down low and then stuff my hands in my pockets and I turn my face aside. I am not a fool. The more rational part of me does not really expect this world to understand the iconography of their ubiquitous Mr. Smiley Face. I am drawing nearer, trying to navigate with peripheral vision, my face still turned sharply aside, focusing on the metal newspaper box to the right of the doors, allowing the guard a benign interpretation of my refusal to look at him. "Evening," I say and then, cleverly, I refer to the newspaper headline which I want him to believe has entranced me. "'Fear and Hope at the End of the Millennium.' How often those two things go together, do they not?"

He makes no reply but neither does he try to stop me. I have already stepped onto the rubber pad and the doors swing open with a sound like the one that admits me to the life-giving atmosphere of my home craft from the vacuum of space. I cross the threshold, I am inside one of Earth's cathedrals of consumerism and the lights dazzle me and I glance quickly about and see no creatures and I duck my head and put on my Groovy Glasses with the dark lenses, affixing my Snappy Sports Strap at the back to hold them on me in the absence of anything quite like earth creatures' ears on my head. I thrust my hands back into my pockets and head off into an empty space to my right, away from the presence of store clerks and any of my fellow shoppers. But even as I avoid them, I am thrilled with the idea of them: my fellow shoppers.

Music plays from above. I'm Bluer Than Blue. How ironic. I am whatever is the opposite of that sentiment. I am redder than red. But now there is a metallic clash of shopping carts nearby and I am yellower than yellow, dashing forward, away from the sound, past a great silver case radiating heat, full of whole rotisserie chickens, and past tables Where it Costs Less to Get More, tables spilling over with French bread and cream cakes and angel-food cakes and cinnamon cakes and Special Sale Half Price fruit cakes and past bins of Big Savings on tubes of Christmas wrapping paper and bags of bows, and the sound that frightened me has ceased. It was the late-night work of some bag boy rounding up the evening's stray carts, I am sure. And now I am in the vast and deserted pharmacy space and I slow down and I am alone and I am happy and I stop and I am standing before rows of mouthwash and they are full of motif and reprise: blue mint and cool mint and peppermint and soft mint and freshmint and my head is spinning with a strange delight and I stagger a bit farther and now there are many ways to hold your false teeth in your head, a matter about which this world is as deeply sympathetic and attentive as the most wonderful and loving father or mother. One can cling, in one's prosthetic vulnerability, to Dentrol and Sea Bond and Fixodent and Poli-Grip and Dentu-Grip and ORAfix and effergrip and Rigident and Cushion Grip and Klutch. I am quaking now with an irrational hope. For what I do not know.

I take off my sunglasses to see all these things in their natural light. My eyes throb for a moment with the brightness, but I adjust. I adjust. I am happy to be here. I am awash in a sense of the possibility of things. Another few steps and there are so many ways to clean one's teeth, one of them Age-Defying. That is all I need from this section. I turn a corner. To stand against the dark stellar wind of mortality, a tube of toothpaste held valiantly before you: perhaps this is the powerful outer edge of yearning.

And now I am among the lipsticks and foundations and blushes and fingernail polishes and mascaras and powders, women set in cardboard all about me, their heads thrown back in perpetual smiles, defiant smiles, it seems to me, rich in Body Fantasies that Make a Statement with the Color of Vibrant Life that Stays on You and Only You. Yes these women, too, are facing the specter of physical decay that confronts all the creatures on this planet—and on my planet, too—on every inhabited planet in the known universe—and these women throw their heads back and laugh and they smile and they are confident and I am standing in the middle of this place, learning so much, and I turn and a woman's face— at first I see it as a face from the racks of cosmetics, but I am wrong—a woman's face, drawn and plain and washed pale as death from the fluorescent lights, turns and sees mine, a tube of Maybelline Great Lash Waterproof mascara in her hand, and her eyes widen at the sight of me and I am suddenly keenly aware of my sunglasses in my hand and she screams.

"Hi," I say. "My name is Desi."

She screams again. There are voices from the other side of the store. Away from my spaceship, on this planet's surface, I could alter the consciousness of only one, perhaps two, creatures at once in, at most, a three-pace radius. I take a step toward this woman who raises her tube of mascara before her, as if it were a weapon. "I am a friendly guy," I say, but she is opening her mouth to scream once more and I quickly wave my hand. She goes glassy-eyed and yawns and smacks her lips, looking about her.

"Hi," she says to no one in particular. "I know a little song."

The other voices, shouting, are coming nearer. I hear a man cry, "It came from over there."

"Three little fishies," the woman before me begins to sing.

I put my Groovy Glasses on and I back away, feeling the heat of panic spreading down my arms and into my hands. I realize my visit to Kroger has come to an end. And things could become much worse than that, as well. Much worse. I hear the electric doors whoosh open in the distance. More voices. The guard has rushed in, I know. I move away quickly, away from the door for the moment, back to the turning I made into the cosmetics aisle and then I go up the cross aisle, keeping low, moving deeper into the store, fleeing the gathering of Earthlings but not without the stiff hot fear of trapping myself. I turn again, my Chuck Taylors making a terrible racket beneath me. I can only hope that my pursuers will split up in their search and that they will not have torches and dogs, and I am in the full flowering of panic now, I realize. I am squeaking along among great bundles of disposable baby diapers, Huggies and Pampers, and I wish for that now, very badly, to be in my wife Edna Bradshaw's arms and she will huggy me and pamper me and we will be safe in the middle of the air and I wish to catch no one up in the clouds ever again. Let this world be.

I am approaching the western wall of the store. Bins again before me, tree stands and Christmas lights and plug-in nativity scenes, though given my circumstances, I am less enchanted now with the Incredible Holiday Savings available here. Sadly, all that matters at this moment is that I must turn right toward the front of the store or left toward the back or retrace my steps. I go to the left, there are less than a dozen more paces to the far corner, but up ahead I see a door and I rush. I had a good plan after all. This will take me into a storage room and then perhaps—almost certainly—a delivery door out the back of the building.

A sign is there: NOT A PUBLIC EXIT. But I am prepared to defy this sign, and I welcome the implication of still another exit— a PRIVATE one—through this way. *Private* is what I deeply desire. And I arrive and I grasp the handle and I turn it and it will not yield. I turn the handle hard and the door is metal and the lock is heavy-duty and I am ill-equipped for the use of physical force. I am heating up again. I spin around and I am trapped in the farthest corner of this vast place, the rows and rows and rows stacking up before my eyes ablaze in fluorescence, blocking my escape, sealing my doom, the voices are drawing nearer, though they are distinct now, separate.

I am amidst the monstrous ironies of pet foods. Against the western wall are stacks of bags of seed to feed sweet little beloved pet birds and next to them rows of cans of murdered bird flesh to feed sweet little beloved pet cats. I am at this moment, needless to say, deeply troubled by the contradictions of life on this planet. Especially as I see the top of a head skimming above a row not far down the way. Skimming in my direction.

Before me, in the space usually assigned to sales bins, are stacks of massive dog-food bags. I step forward and I crouch down low behind them. I wait for a moment and I peek around the bags and my vision is filled with roach killers. Roach Motels, in fact, with a tiny, welcoming facade on each package, and an open door, but it is clear to any objective eye that this is a trap. They Check In But They Do Not Check Out.

I duck back behind my dog food in a significantly worsened state of mind. I need to stop thinking now, but emblazoned over and over on my bastion of bags is BUTCHER'S CHOICE. And I see my too-many fingers and toes being chopped off and scraped from the cutting block with the steaming blade, not enough meat here even for dog food, and all my loving digits drop into a garbage box, and now the blade lifts to lop off this similarly useless head, its lipless smile still fixed there, even in death.

Ironically, though the words on these very bags themselves have prompted this final twist of fear in me, in response I scrunch up even harder against them, trying to compact myself into a very small object, half-price and useless to anyone, easily overlooked.

But there is a quick scuffling sound heading this way and a figure suddenly in my sight, off to my left, trying the door that I tried, finding it, as I did, locked. And now the figure turns, a very young man in a Kroger shirt the color of clotting blood, and he has a name tag, which calms me a little bit, though it is not nearly as friendly a tag as my wife Edna Bradshaw's. Simply: KROGER *Roger*. And Roger sees me and I am a strange sight to his eyes, he is struck dumb, but my sunglasses are still on and he is not sure what it is he is seeing, though strange it is. This is fortunate. He takes a step toward me without yet making a sound and I wave my hand and he stops and his eyelids droop and his body does a slow ooze to the floor and he is asleep.

I wonder how many are in pursuit of me. The staff must be small at this hour. And there would be no need for everyone in the store to join in. After all, there is still commerce to do. And they would have gotten no help in focusing on their target from the woman whose scream began it all. Indeed, they might be on the lookout for three little fishies.

But now I hear a clear "Oh my God," a man's voice, and rushing feet and the voice again: "Over here." I look toward Roger and at the moment I do, a large white mass descends and hovers over the sleeping young man. And from it, a face turns and the eyes there widen. The body twists my way. Another Kroger name tag. *Ken*.

Ken the *assistant manager*. I wave my hand at Ken and he is snoring even before he sinks forward, which he does, quickly, ending
up pressed on top of Roger, the two men's faces cheek-to-cheek.

Someone is calling out "Ken" now. I creep forward, closer to
the sleepers. Ken's torso, clad in his immaculate white shirt, is firmly
at rest against Roger, but he is still on his knees and his rear end is
stuck in the air. He looks uncomfortable. But I do not help him
into a better posture for sleeping. I remain hidden behind the dog
food and another scuffling of feet is coming this way, another man's
voice. "Ken," the voice says. "What the hell are you doing?" More
scuffling and then, "Oh shit."

I hear the crackle of a two-way radio. This must be the guard.
And he is calling for help from the local authorities. "This is Nate,"
he says. "We got ourselves a problem. Over."

I rise up and peek over the top of the dog food. It is indeed
the man in the tan uniform. He is looking down at the two sleepers and he takes a step toward them. I lift my hand and he says
into his radio, "I'm not sure . . ." and then he sees me and adds—
not exactly into his radio but generally, for Ken and Roger and Barry
Manilow, who is singing overhead about trying to get some un-
named feeling again—"Oh fuck me." And I realize that my Groovy
Glasses are in my hand again and I do not even remember taking
them off. Nate is surely about to say more, even though his face
seems frozen in its contemplation of mine, but I do not give him
the chance. I wave my hand and the radio clatters to the floor,
spitting out static and broken cries for someone to come back. But
Nate himself is settling down to sleep, ignoring the upthrust of
Ken's backside, drooping down against the delicate balance of the
assistant manager so that he topples sideways and I am left with a
stack of three loudly snoring members of this planet's primary
species at my feet. I look quickly around and I see no more gliding

heads, hear no more rushing feet. But the radio is crackling in the center of the aisle and I must assume that a police car is on its way.

I wave my hand over each of the three sleepers to ensure they will have no memory of me and I rush off as fast as my sneakers will carry me, back in the direction of the door, the profusion of goods flowing past me on each side in an indistinguishable blur. I think of Ken and Roger and Nate and wonder what they will conclude when they wake and find themselves intertwined on the floor with no memory of how they arrived there. Perhaps love will inadvertently bloom. I wish for that as I rush past the woman who began all this and her voice carries me toward the automatic door: "Swim little fishies, swim if you can . . ."

I am released, thankfully, from the fluorescence and into the darkness and already I hear a siren, and I turn toward the open space of ROLLER RINK, which seems to me a very great distance away. I take a step and another and another and I lean forward, into the night, trying to glide the best I can, but as much as I admire my Chuck Taylors, they are not made to facilitate the movement of a member of my species and I press forward, across the asphalt, under the glare of a light and into darkness again and the siren is drawing nearer and I am moving with agonizing slowness and I realize what an obviously suspicious figure I make in my hat and my trench coat and my size-twenty yellow sneakers and I realize I have to remove them, the sneakers, I am no longer concerned about a part of my body giving away my true identity, I am concerned only with running fast from the coppers, who are drawing ever nearer. So I begin pulling at one of my sneakers even as I try to keep my forward momentum and the Chuck Taylor clings to me and I am hopping on one foot with the other in my hands and I hop and wrench at my sneaker and hop and wrench and hop and I am a Bad Boy and I am wondering what I am going to do because the authorities are unquestionably coming for me and I am not sure if I can control the situation.

And over my shoulder I hear the train whistle once more, quite loud, as if it, too, is in pursuit of me, and there is another sound, a clackity-clack and I look and the train is passing in front of Kroger, slowly, approaching the crossing and there are red lights flashing there and I can see the blue and white flashing of police lights racing this way from the street along the tracks and the engine reaches the crossing and enters it and its cars are following and beneath them I can see the flare of blue and white approach and slow and turn to come to get me. But the police vehicle is blocked there by the train. And I hop on along, still clinging to one determinedly sneakered foot. I hop across the street and through the ghost-space of Roller Rink and I bounce along to my invisible craft and I am at last passing inside and I release my foot and I move to the controls and I sit before them, and I pause. I look toward Kroger and I am filled with regret for causing upset in a Family Center. But there is far more upset to come, I fear. Far more. And I move my hand and I rise above Lake Charles, Louisiana, quickly, and I fly toward the huggies of my wife.

12

Edna Bradshaw was still sleeping when I returned. Everyone on the ship was sleeping. But when I lay down beside my wife, she stirred without opening her eyes and her arms came around me as if she knew in her very dreams what it was that I needed at that moment. I was grateful.

I am frightened. Even lying here now with my wife Edna Bradshaw's arms about me, even with a fetching scent of something coming from her, a good scent that seems to come straight from her knockers, which tower above me in her embrace and which are so unlike anything among my species, even with all of that, I can think only of my imminent public appearance on this planet, how it will be fraught with danger and needs a careful plan, and how even the vague first glimmerings of such a plan are still far from my mind. I continue to believe that whatever I am to do, whatever I am to say, has to be shaped by all the voices of creatures, alive and dead, floating in the vast energy fields of my memory machines and, more to the present point, all the voices now sleeping on my ship and ready to speak. These latter voices are surely as close as I can get to the exact tenor of this particular era, the fin de siècle state of consciousness of the creatures I will face in vast numbers in a very short time.

And so, without letting go to further sleep myself, I gently disengage from my wife's arms and I rise and enter into the corridor and as I move toward the place where they are all waiting I let myself try to calculate exactly how much time I have before I must descend from my machine in plain sight.

It is not an easy calculation to do in one's head.

My time is not their time.

And I am surely wrong in doing a thing like this without my machines.

And I stagger to a stop.

I have gotten close to a bottom line but I have averted my eyes at the last moment, professing ignorance, feigning ignorance, hoping for ignorance, and I move off now to our control room and I am before my machines and I am a simple movement of my hand away from having the precise answer and I am Hot as a Firecracker and Ready to Explode. I am also having trouble drawing a breath. The hand I finally move is a slab of rock, a layer hacked from a desert excavation full of the fossils of life on this planet long ago dead.

And my eyes try to see the numbers that appear before me as if they are hieroglyphs from an extinct language. Unreadable. But this cannot last for long. My mind peeks. And the heat in me swells and roils. I knew it was not long, the time left to me. But the numbers before me are a terrible surprise.

I have twenty-two hours and eleven minutes.

I envy the roaches of the planet Earth. I am ready to check in, quite willingly, to a place where I cannot check out.

But I am who I am.

And this is my life.

And there are so many voices to hear before I offer myself up.

And so I go out of the control room and I move again in the corridors of my spaceship, move quickly, and I am among my visitors—I realize now that I may not have a chance to hear them all—

and so I choose the visitor whose very name derives from what all of these sojourners were seeking on their bus when I caught them up in the clouds, a thing that I, too, seek for myself. I awaken, to a state of dreamspeak, the young man named Lucky.

He sits before me now and I am—I hear how *words* create their own states of being and this one I wish were true—I am Lucky. *I am an all-American guy, through and through red white and blue, and that is the fact. I don't even remember Vietnam. Not even a little bit. My mother and father, they talk about it all the time while I am growing up. You should have seen the clouds in the sky at twilight. You should have seen the teakwood furniture in our house. You should have seen the Emperor of Jade pagoda. And I say, Right. You should see the Astros play the Cardinals. Maybe you can get lucky and see Mark McGwire hit a home run. I go to one game this past season and he hits a ball about ten rows into the upper deck. I root for the Astros but I like to see big home runs and this one was about as big as they get.*

See, even my name is Lucky. I could call myself Joe or Ed or Bill or anything I want since I am an American and since my parents gave me a Vietnamese name. I don't blame them, understand, I was born in Vietnam and all, but things went bad over there, as everybody knows, and my parents and my sister and me ended up running away. And you can't carry your teakwood furniture on a sampan stuffed full of refugees in the South China Sea. So we came to the USA with basically the clothes on our backs—realize, I don't have a single memory of any of this—and then at some point it became clear that the communist government wasn't just going to up and topple over and we were pretty much stuck here—stuck is how my parents saw it—and they realized it was time for me to have a name that my fellow Americans would understand. So they let me choose. It was when I was twelve years old.

Knowing how they feel about what they lost, that must have been a bad day for them. We all of us sat around our kitchen table in our little condo out in the Bellaire part of Houston and we had a stack of name-your-baby books and we all chose new names. Our family name was Nguyễn. For sure, nobody American could say that. But when people tried and just chose to duck that Ng sound at the start, they often ended up saying something that sounded like an American name: Wynn. So my father made the family name first order of business and that's what he said it was going to be. Wynn. Which was fine by me. I was already a baseball fan and I knew about my Astros even back to when they were the Colt 45s, before I was born, and one of the early Astros greats was Jimmy Wynn, who hit ninety-six home runs in the three seasons from '67 to '69. He was a little guy and they called him the Toy Cannon. I like to think of him all through those bad years of the war out there in the air-conditioned comfort of the Astro- dome, this little man, getting just his pitch, guessing just right on the fastball or the curve ball and he'd swing and be right on the money, right on the sweet spot on his bat, not a millimeter off—there is some guesswork to good hitting, you see; it takes some luck to hit the long ball—I like to think of him hitting big home runs in 1967 and 1968 and 1969 and him jogging around the bases, not having to rush because everything was already decided in his favor. It was like he was preparing a place for me. I'm sorry for my parents and what they lost and its never being okay for them, but Jimmy Wynn was lay- ing down this track for a guy who looked to be Vietnamese but ended up an American, cheering his Astros and free to chase his own luck. Me.

So my sister goes first on that day and she doesn't even look in the books. She's fifteen and it's clear she's been thinking about this for a long time, probably been wanting to ask my parents for this very thing but she's too good and obedient and old-fashioned a daughter to open her mouth. She even claims to remember the furniture and the sunsets some, back in Vietnam. Nancy, she says.

Nancy? I say. From Nancy Reagan?

This is after almost four years of Ronald in the White House, 1986, the year the Astros finished ten games ahead in the Western Division and then lost to the Mets in the playoffs. Real bad luck. And the Mets go on and win the World Series that year only because a guy lets a slow, good-hop ground ball go through his legs, a ball he's going to catch nine hundred and ninety-nine times out of a thousand. And because of that, the Red Sox don't win the World Series, which they hadn't for seventy years and they still haven't, to this day. One chance in a thousand they lose in 1986 and that's their luck.

So my sister says, Yes, I admire her.

I also, says my father, who wants this to go smoothly. That is a good choice, he says.

Then my dad says, Fred.

Is that you? I say.

That is me, he says.

Is that from Fred Flintstone? I say. Which is this cartoon character caveman.

And my father gets angry. You do not take this in the right spirit, he says to me. It is plenty hard already, all these things that happen to us. You are spoiled child. You are not Vietnamese at all.

He says this last thing like it's going to hurt my feelings, like I'm going to get upset about it. But of course I'm not Vietnamese. I don't want to be. I'm on another team now. The ball went through my father's legs and that was that. Bad luck.

My mother is flipping through the name books and she can't stand it, my father and me fighting, so she starts calling out names for herself, though she's not being too choosy, which tells me she's just trying to stop the two of us.

How about Hildegarde, she says.

My father's head snaps in her direction at this.

But she's going on before he can say anything. Maybe Hyacinth, she says.

It should go with Fred, my father says, but his voice is suddenly tiny like he just realized he missed the ball. It's dribbling into right field and he's blown it for everybody.

My mother looks up from the book and straight into his eyes. She thinks a moment and turns Fred over silently in her mouth, you can see her shaping it. It's just a word, after all. Just a stupid word. It's not going to change who either of them is. And then she says, Ethel.

And she's serious.

I'd watched some episodes of that old TV show with the screwy whiney wife of the good-natured dodo of a Cuban band leader. Lucy and Desi. And they had these friends, an old miser and a sort of screwy whiney wife assistant. Fred and Ethel. Fred was a geezer. He looked to be about thirty years older than Ethel. They didn't have any kids, and the only thing interesting to me about them was thinking he married her when he was probably forty-five and she was about fifteen and she's been waiting decades for him to come through for her some night, but he never does. With that situation running unspoken under the surface, it made everything else really kind of interesting. But there I sit looking from my mother to my father and back again. From Ethel to Fred to Ethel. And I just keep my mouth shut about it.

But it turns out later that my father chose Fred from some big boss he'd never even spoken a word to at Pennzoil. My father is a computer expert there. He hates computers. And my mother chose Ethel from hearing somewhere that Fred and Ethel were some kind of couple, but she didn't know anything else about them. So when my mother says,

Ethel, my father goes, Good. My sister goes, Good, and she's not even trying to keep from laughing or anything, though she knows the TV show as well as I do. It sounds like she really does believe those names are good, which is a pretty scary thing about my sister, if you stop and consider it.

And now they're all three looking at me.

Not that I haven't also given this a lot of thought already. So I say, Lucky.

My father says, Lucky? What kind of name is that, Lucky?

I'm ready for him. I say, It's the English translation of my Vietnamese name.

And what I said was true. My Vietnamese given name was Vận. Of course, right away my mother and father know I've got them.

I say, I want to keep this connection to my beginnings in Vietnam. And I look over at my sister, Nancy Reagan Wynn, who's supposed to be the one that appreciates our family's roots, and she knows I got her, too.

That is very good, my mother says. I give you lucky name myself.

My father can't quite make himself say the words, but he's got no choice except to nod his approval, in spite of his suspicions about me.

My sister says, You sure it's not from Lucky Luciano? Wasn't he a gangster who got whacked in a barber chair?

I'm surprised at you, Nancy, I say, making my voice sound hurt. I even think she's got that wrong. Lucky Luciano died of old age.

Or maybe Lucky Strikes, my sister says.

I've really gotten to her.

They'll give you cancer, she says.

I even force a faint sob into my voice. I say to her, I thought you'd be the first to understand how I miss my real home.

Yes, my mother says to my sister, watch how you talk.

So I get what I want. I get my luck, right there in my name. And it's even at the expense of the one perfect Vietnamese child in the family.

And I am lucky. I'm twenty-five years old and I'm making ninety grand a year in computers. I love computers. I've got a great girl, Mary Wynn—no relation, fortunately—and her original name was Hiện, which means generous, and she is that, she's a generous girl who loves me. And I get to go to the casino boats and do what I love the most, next to watching the Astros. Well, maybe even more than watching the Astros, because this is more like playing the game, not just watching it.

I play the slots. A lot of Vietnamese go to gamble. They even have a Vietnamese night once a month at one of the boats, with some Vietnamese singer or other whining out sorrowful tunes for a room full of exiles. They're not so different from me, really. Except they're most of them looking to get something back. They got unlucky once, in a big way. Drew one too many cards and lost a country. And it gave them a big dose of gambler's logic: you lose that big and things have got to turn your way just as big, the great cosmic odds tables have got to work themselves out. Even better if it's in a different currency. Lose a country, win a million bucks. But you got to be on the spot when the time for that adjustment comes or you just end up a big loser forever and you've done it to yourself.

I understand where they're coming from. And they all love the card tables. Blackjack and baccarat and Pai Gow poker, which is pretty funny if you think about it, Vietnamese gamblers trying to win back their pasts playing a Chinese game. But like I say, it's the slots for me. The megabucks dollar slots.

One on one, pitcher and batter, facing that next moment of your life. That's what it is for me. I'm not trying to make up for anything. I don't figure the universe is ready to even my score. It's just me and the moment. And I always use the handle on the machine. No punching buttons. You punch a button, it's like you're entirely passive. You're just saying, I'm ready. Show me what you've got. That's okay as far as it

*goes. But with the handle, you've got a chance to play the moment. You
know? You palm that black ball at the end and you curl your fingers
around it and you wait. You can feel the time slipping along and you're
going to do this thing and you're either going to lose or you're going to
win. But there's a way to make it your own. I'm sure of it. Like thinking,
Okay, he's shown me his curveball low and outside twice, now he's
going to try to bust a fastball inside. I'm guessing fastball and I'm ready
for it. There's four clicks on the handle. You can hear them, and if there's
too much noise—that loud, steady, Saturday-night casino roar—then
you can feel them in the palm of your hand. One click. Two. You're doing
this slow and counting them. Three. Four. And you pause, maybe. Or
you don't. However it is you're feeling this thing at the moment. There's
this flow of time and if you jump in at one particular second you win
and if you jump in at another second you lose. That's the way things
are. So you feel click number four, and you hold one beat, two—and the
progressive is quietly counting away over your head, five million and
something dollars and something cents, and it's running up fast, busy
storing up a fortune for you, and you wait for that third beat, and that's
it, you realize, a little waltz here, three-four time, and you take your
swing.*

*And what you're waiting for is three little eagles. That's all. In the
window of the slot machine. Forget the minor scores, the singles and
doubles and triples, the cherries and the bars and the sevens. You're going
for the upper deck. You wait for three little red white and blue eagles to
land side by side for you. Look where you are, they'll say to me. It's
America.*

Lucky Wynn and I stop speaking. He is suspended now,
waiting, I think, for the eagles to line up in the window of a slot
machine in his head. And I am, too. I keep pulling the handle and
I am waiting for some of these voices to line up side by side—per-

haps it will only take three of them—and they will say, Look where you are. And I will know. But inevitably, there is only one voice before me and a blank on either side.

This I do understand. Lucky knows as little as I do. He says he is American, but I think there are feelings in him that he is not recognizing. He is still waiting—yearning—to be this thing he thinks he already is, to learn these things he thinks he already knows.

A lost home. A vessel that carries you away to another place. A new name. Others around you whose voices you hear but that you do not truly understand. Nor do they truly understand you. I share this diaspora with Lucky Wynn. But even knowing this, I can think of nothing to do or to say to him, except lead him back to his place so that he can return to sleep. And, eventually, to return him to his life, the memory of all this erased, and his yearning will go on.

But, of course, there may be no need to erase the memories of any of my present visitors, since I will myself follow them back to this planet's surface and will reveal the secret to everyone. In only a matter of hours now. Let them all remember.

And I do lead Lucky back to the deep shadows of his sleeping space and then I stand in the corridor and I listen to the breathing of all of my visitors as they sleep and wait. I need to push on to the next voice. There may yet be some sudden revelation. But I do not know how to choose and so I begin to pace up and down the corridor outside these doorways and I sing to myself. I need to do this anyway. I sing a wordless song inside me—and I mean by using this word *sing* something other than the thing meant by music on the planet below me, for this song is not translated into elements— words, perceivable sounds—that can exist in the shared physical space outside one's internal landscape—these are primal tones rising and spinning inside me like the crepuscular spirals of dust and cloud and moisture on my home planet, a process that nightly comes with the setting of our beautiful blue star, the very elements of our world rising up to bid our star farewell, rising up in their yearning—yes, I now readily attribute this condition even to the inanimate substances of my own planet—they yearn to go with that star as it seems about to leave us all alone. This is the sensual theme of the song I sing, a song created in my own head, even as I sing it, existing only there in its true form, like no one else's song, and I, too, yearn, I yearn to place this music into the head of a being other than myself, directly, untranslated, but my own wife Edna Bradshaw, whom I love with a great spiral of feeling inside me, my own wife cannot hear this kind of music, I cannot share it with her, and I know this is true of all the beings on this planet, it is how they live: If there is some deep sense of an essential thing inside them, an ontological music, beyond words, beyond sounds, it is impossible for them truly to share it with anyone else.

I have let my thoughts grow intrusive now. The music stops. I stop. I am before a sleeping space and so I choose this one. And soon we are in the speaking place. Sitting before me is the tiny, elderly form of Viola Stackhouse. And though she cannot place the things that are inside her directly inside me, we do speak as one, we shape these words as one. *My husband Arthur buys Buicks. He always has. He says the Buick LeSabre was the one American car they never forgot how to build, even in the bad days of the late seventies and into the eighties, when the Japanese came and took over our car market because so many of the US makers seemed to forget how to do it right.*

And you know, it's always been an uncomfortable thing for me, his love of Buicks. All these years I'd rather be riding around in just about any kind of car except a Buick. But what could I say? There's no way for a wife to even begin to explain a crazy thing like that to her husband. It was just a feeling. Whenever it's come time to trade our car in—about every two or three years, Arthur loves to trade in a car with no more than forty thousand miles on it for a new one—when it's come time, I've always tried to suggest this car or that instead. But it's his thing, you know. It's something he's done all his life, always Buicks, which I guess he got from his father. When better automobiles are built, Buick will build them, Arthur has always said to me. And what could I say to that? "Please don't, I've got this unexplainable aversion to every car you've ever bought"?

But sitting here now, I suddenly remember. Pretty clearly, though it's been a long time. Is that a bad sign? Am I about to die or something? Or is it just senility? Whichever, there's this one thing that comes back to me. A 1929 model Buick. My mama was going to leave my papa and she and her boyfriend and I, we all of us got in the boyfriend's 1929 Buick roadster to drive to Reno for her to get the divorce. They lifted me into the rumble seat—I was, what, five years old, I guess—and we took off from in front of the Hotel Senator in Sacramento, where my mama and I were staying temporarily, and she wrapped me up in the chenille spread she got off the hotel bed. It was a morning in the middle of October and the weather was pretty nice. It wasn't very cold out. I was swaddled up and I know I didn't like her boyfriend, exactly, but I didn't hate him, even though I knew what was going on here.

It was my mama I loved the most, she was with me all the time and I was aware even then that I didn't see my papa very often, though I think that was from him trying to make money and not from running around with other women. Over the years, as an adult, when I thought about what happened between my mother and father, I always came to that conclusion. And Mama said this was okay, what was happening, and though of course I wanted things to be settled and normal, in the way any child wants her family to be, as long as I was with her and she was saying it was okay, I wasn't as unhappy about the breakup as you might expect.

He was my father's business partner. They were stock brokers together in their own little firm in San Francisco, where we lived. And they were both of them the same kinds of damn fools as the rest of the country through the twenties, playing a high-stakes game and thinking you never had to fold your hand and walk away. Though listen to me. I love to gamble. Maybe not love it. I get something I need out of gambling and I keep doing it. But at least I know how much I'm ready to lose, and when I lose it, I know how to find my way to the door.

But none of this about the situation is new to me. I had plenty of time growing up and being an adult to think out the issues and all of how things went in my family, how my mama divorced my papa and she went on to a life of, more or less, chaos after that. I'm getting off what it is that just came to me. What's new in my recollection is the drive to Reno, and that Buick. He had a Buick and I was wrapped in a bedspread and my mama and her boyfriend were in front of me, the backs of their heads, in the roadster's main seat and I was in the rumble seat and they paid me no attention at all. She snuggled up to him and he put his arm around her and it was like I wasn't there at all. It was just me and the Buick.

And that was fine. It was a wonderful car. I can see that. My mama's boyfriend had paid maybe fifteen hundred dollars for it, which was enough to support two families for a whole year back then. And I think the seat was leather and it was more comfortable than our couch at home. And I could hear the Buick's motor. Most of the cars in the street made a terrible racket, sputtering and burbling and coughing away. But this Buick purred. Even idling at a corner while my mama and her boyfriend waited too long having a kiss and somebody behind us would honk his horn and yell. Even then, the Buick was making this low, smooth sound, right underneath me, it felt like, and all the other stuff didn't concern me. The Buick was holding me tight and talking to me low and sweet and then it carried me away, fast, making the wind blow in my hair.

My word. I loved that Buick, didn't I. This doesn't explain a thing. The Buick carried me into a quiet, green world, meadows and folds of land and fields filled with low growing things, vegetables I knew, but I could name nothing, no vegetable, no tree, no fold or lift of land, I had no words at that age to name anything. Except the jagged edge of mountains before me—I knew those were the High Sierras—my mother's boyfriend had told me this name before we began—and we rose to them and the Buick whispered to me, reassured me, carried me up and into a forest and we rose gradually, for miles and miles, and the road began to twist and turn and I was okay with all of this. I saw, once, among the trunks of the trees, the dappled flank of a deer and, briefly, its dark eyes. I was something like happy.

But it was getting cold. The sun was there, free and clear in the sky, and yet, even as it seemed to get brighter as we climbed, it gave off less and less heat. I wondered at this. I began to tremble with the cold. I hunched into the seat, pulled the bedspread tighter around me, but it was a thin thing, I realized, there was so much of it wrapped around me that you'd think it would make anyone warm, but it was very thin and as pitiful as the sun. I looked at my mother and her boyfriend and they were snuggled close and they did not seem to notice the cold at all. And the Buick was carrying me and whispering still and I wanted it to warm me, as well, but it could not.

Then we were over the top and we began to descend and suddenly the world changed. It was all rock and dust and scrawny things growing and patches of grass that hunkered low and looked like the scum between the tiles in our bathroom. And I was trembling and the road was sharply angled and I could look down for what seemed like miles, down these long folds of barren rock, and I felt like there was something gripping me by the shoulders and wanting to pluck me from the seat and throw me down this mountain and I pressed myself down, tried to make myself as heavy as a boulder, and I asked the Buick to please not let me go. And it didn't. The Buick held me and it held to the road and it wound us down the mountain and the air was growing warmer and I was listening carefully again to the Buick's voice and I was okay.

And then there was a catch in the voice. The engine coughed and stammered and coughed again and my mama's boyfriend cursed and I suddenly was aware of the road and it was angled sharply down and there was a great dome of rock off one way and a sharp drop the other way and the road was narrow and the Buick shuddered a little and I said to it, softly, No. Please. But the engine fell quiet and the brakes whined and the boyfriend cursed some more and my mama was making little gasping sounds and I didn't care about those two at all, not at all, I spread my hands out from under the bedspread and I laid them flat on the Buick's leather seat and I prayed for the car to come back to life, to carry me on to a place where I'd be safe and everything would be okay forever.

But we rolled through a curve and then another and my mama was saying her boyfriend's name over and over and he was telling her to shut up and then there was a little bit of a gravelly shoulder to the road at a curve coming up and it was very narrow and there was a sharp edge beyond it and then a big break in things, a leap, the next thing out that you could see was about a mile away, and you could feel the boyfriend stomp on the brakes, put everything he could into them, and we swerved onto the shoulder and there was a great spitting of gravel beneath us and my mama screamed and then we stopped.

They didn't say a thing for a while in the front, though you could hear them breathing hard. They were sitting apart, my mama and her boyfriend, and looking opposite ways. Me, I sat listening to the Buick. It was making a little ticking sound. Then it stopped even that. I was sitting in the center of the rumble seat and I pulled the bedspread from

around me and crept to the right, keeping my face low at first, smelling
the leather of the Buick's upholstery, thinking, What a phony you are,
what a phony, what good is it that you smell nice. And then I was ready
and I lifted my head up and I looked out, and there was only a great and
wide chasm before me, gray and rocky and deep, and this was what all
the holding and the carrying and the sweet low whispering was about.
Just to bring me to the edge of the rest of my life and fall silent.

Funny. I don't remember much of anything else from that trip.
Things sort of stop there on the mountain. Obviously somebody came
along and we made it to Reno. I do know the divorce didn't happen that
fall. That much I've been told. We were supposed to live in a hotel there
for three months to establish residency, but it got cut short. Somewhere
in the first week or two the stock market crashed and my father and his
partner, my mama's boyfriend, were both ruined. So were Mama and
me, in a certain way. So was pretty much everybody.

Now that explains it, I guess, about Buicks. To me at least. To a
sympathetic googly-eyed alien, I guess. But it would never do for Arthur.
He'd never understand. I'm just happy he knows when to fold a losing
hand and find his way to the door. We both do. That makes for an okay
marriage, it seems to me.

I have ceased being Viola Stackhouse. Before me, her eyes close
for a moment as she decompresses from her memory. Then she
looks at me and says, "Did I offend you?"

"Of course not," I say.

"Didn't I just call you a googly-eyed alien?" she says.

"Ah yes," I say. "But a *sympathetic* googly-eyed alien."

"Didn't I scream a lot, too? At the little party you and your
wife threw for us?"

"You were afraid for Arthur."

"This is all new," she says. "I never saw this coming."

"Not even in the High Sierras," I say.

She smiles at this. "You're not offended? At how I've been acting?"

"No."

"My mama had quite a few boyfriends over the years. I'd not call one of them *sympathetic*."

"Or googly-eyed," I say.

"Maybe one or two of them was that, toward the end." Viola Stackhouse laughs.

Then her laugh breaks off and I know she is sitting on the edge of the great and wide chasm of what her life has been and I take her hands in mine and I touch her with my fingertips and I give her the beating of my heart.

"Oh my," she says.

"Prepare for sleep now," I whisper, trying to make my voice as deep and smooth as a Buick.

And I take her back to her place and I help her lie down and I wish very badly to have a chenille spread to wrap her in, but there is only so much that I can do, and perhaps it is all right, for she is already asleep.

It has been a long night. But my time is short. And I am a late-night gambler juiced on the thrill of the game. I have pulled the handle on the slot machine over and over and now I have a red white and blue eagle in the left-hand window and the other windows are still tumbling and I wait for the second eagle to fall into place. I need a big win and I need it soon. Then I have an idea I should have had before: speak to the mated pairs one after the other. So I awaken Arthur and he is sitting before me now. I am Viola's husband. I am Arthur Stackhouse. *I saw some pretty bad things in the war. I'm talking about the real war. The good war. But I basically* came out of it with a free mind. It helped that we all knew it was for a righteous cause, which included our own families' welfare. It really did. You knew in your bones that every wife and child in America, every mailbox and apple tree, was at stake. And it helped, too, somehow, to know you were in for the duration. None of this twelve-months-and-you're-gone stuff, which I figure made it even worse for the boys in that other war, the dirty one, a couple of decades later. If you go to war and it's not for anything you can see as important, no matter how much rhetoric they throw at you, and if you're going to be out of the action in one year, win or lose, then it just has to make a big difference in your being able to deal with it. You never quite get safely into that place inside you that will let you kill and be killed.

Now, I don't know any of that about the Vietnam War and the boys who went there, except as a bystander. That's just how I figured it was, from what I read and saw on TV. But what I'm really trying to talk about here is myself, how I could go through what I did in France and Germany and then come back and put it out of my mind better than you might expect. My generation, after you got home, you never talked about it to anybody, and you held on tight to all the things you loved that you knew would've been seriously harmed if you hadn't done what you did, and that helped make the bad stuff quiet down and eventually go away. So I was all right. For a few years.

Then all of a sudden I wasn't all right. And I never have been since. And damned if it didn't come about in peacetime on a hotel roof with a drink in my hand. Till a few years ago, when Louisiana floated those casinos in Lake Charles, my wife and I would go to Las Vegas twice a year. We did it every year since we were married, which was right after the war, in 1946. And there was a time in the early fifties when the government was doing all that testing of hydrogen bombs out in the desert. It wasn't very many miles away from Vegas, where the testing grounds were, and for a while the casinos made a big promotion of it.

So in 1953 my wife and I were at one of the hotels. The Sahara maybe. Or the Sands. I don't remember which one. But there was a rooftop party to watch a nuclear blast. We both had already lost what we'd budgeted ourselves to lose and we had another twenty-four hours in Vegas and this seemed like something interesting. So we went up and they had Miss Atomic there, who they'd chose in a beauty pageant that morning, and she was walking around in a swimsuit and high heels and she had an atomic hairdo, which was big and puffed up on the top of her head like a mushroom cloud, and they were serving something they called atomic cocktails, which I remember very clearly. It was vodka and brandy and champagne and sherry, the strangest mix of things, but it was pretty good and getting better with every sip I took.

Then it was time and they had one of those tuxedoed emcees from down in the floor showrooms and he was doing like an introduction. It was dusk, I think. That's how I remember it. There was still a little light from the sun that had just disappeared but it was getting dark and this guy is going, Now ladies and gentlemen, playing the Sahara for one night only, the Hydrogen Bomb, let's give him a big Vegas welcome with a round of applause. And then the emcee looks at his watch and starts counting backward from ten and people are applauding and I take a sip of my atomic cocktail and Viola is standing beside me and I'm looking out to the northwest, where the sky is still showing some light.

Then it happened. I wasn't prepared at all. You read about this bomb in the newspapers and it's supposed to have killed all those people in a couple of Japanese towns and so forth, and you see a newsreel in the movies and you watch the mushroom cloud and you think, This is some kind of bomb. Something like that. But all you're doing is just that, thinking. Like thinking about war if you've never been there. You just don't know jack shit. All of a sudden there's this crown of light out there. You know it's sixty, seventy miles away, but all of a sudden it's there, this spray of white light, but it doesn't register as white as all, if you're used *to thinking of whiteness as a clean thing. This is white like you've been wrong all your life about what death is. It's not like closing your eyes and everything is black and that's the way it stays forever. Suddenly you know death is white, and here it is and it doesn't feel far away at all. It's right here in your face, touching your eyes, which don't close when you die but they look straight into this ghastly whiteness.*

And then it fades a little, it pulls back, but something else is there in its place. And damn, you can see it. Even from here. It's tiny from this distance, if you step back and look around you, if you can drag your eyes away and look up at the night sky, but you can't do that. You have to see what's there, and it's a thing rising up where that whiteness was just a moment ago. And more than the worst of battle, more than the smell of cordite or burnt flesh, more than the sound of men's voices blabbering in pain, more than the sight of torn limbs and gaping chests, that instant of light and that distant plume of smoke and the mindless smattering of applause on a hotel rooftop and the taste of champagne and sherry told me there was nothing but pain and then nothingness waiting for me in my life. I was thirty years old and I'd been through a terrible war but it wasn't until that evening I realized what the end of life was all about.

And my wife put her hand on my arm and maybe she knew something terrible was happening inside me and maybe she didn't. But I never said a word about this to her. I kept my battle face on and I sipped my drink and she and I went downstairs and I think I broke our rule that night. I think I lost another hundred dollars or so that we didn't budget, and I knew I'd lose it. There was no way I'd win a penny that night. But I went through the motions. And I guess that did me some good, in a way. I went on through the motions of my life and here I am. And I never did say a thing about this to Viola. She wouldn't understand. Or she would. Either way, we'd lose.

What's wrong with this species? Its individuals seem to be profoundly ignorant of those even closest to them. Damn it, Arthur, speak to Viola. Viola, speak to Arthur. Share the things that are inside you. You are inferior beings. This is all I can think with Arthur Stackhouse dozing exhausted before me. I let him sit like that in the interview chair for a while.

But I am ashamed at these thoughts. Perhaps it is my own weariness that has rendered me immobile and cranky. After all, I have myself repeatedly castigated the inadequacy of *words* in the conduct of life on this planet. The silence between Arthur and Viola is based on their own recognition of the same thing. Is that not sensible on their part?

And perhaps there is even more betokened by this irritability that has come upon me. How can I be critical of this species when a sterling example of my own species, namely myself, Desi the Spaceman, a creature who is not even limited biologically by words, is, in fact, ignorant of himself. Is that not a far greater fault than the one I am finding in others?

This particular moment of ignorance is falling away now. But I am clearly capable of such a failure. I am afraid to consider what other manifestations of that self-ignorance I have been prey to. But for now, for this instance, the part of me that I failed to recognize and that transformed itself into a condemnation of the Stackhouses' species concerns an issue—I am conscious of the irony—that our two species share with more or less equal intensity. An issue that is, typically, hiding behind even these words I now shape.

I speak of death. I speak of death. The ultimate wordlessness. I have not seen it as a whiteness until Arthur and I were one voice. I have always seen it as darkness, the way Arthur once did, though my frame of reference, not surprisingly, was the deep concentration of gravity in space that we have chosen, as a species, never physically to approach. I speak of the black holes. That was the metaphor resident in my head. That our life should cease, our music fall silent: we are terrified of this. Yes. But it has always been like that dreadful suck of darkness, those places where you dared not go. Or, in a different mood, death was the darkness between the stars, the thing we moved in all the time, a commonplace thing, a thing that we could put aside with the mere shifting of our eyes to the stars themselves. The darkness could not exist without the light and was therefore subordinate to it. Subject to it. And even filled with particles. Stellar winds. Whatever. Foolish elaborations of metaphor for the sake of self-delusion.

But Arthur would have me see the stars themselves, the blinding whiteness, as death. And the clear realization of this flares through me and stiffens my fingers and my toes and I try to think of red stars and blue stars, but it does no good, for I understand Arthur, it has nothing to do with the bending of the light into these other hues, they are a deception, they are part of the same vanishing.

I remember a voice. Arthur Stackhouse is sleeping, his head bowed low, his chin nearly touching his chest. I do not disturb him. I move my hand to the control panel and pass it there and I find a voice I myself gathered just a few years ago. Though Arthur Stackhouse sits before me, I am Jacob Klein. *This is the thought I sometimes have. For years, I've had it already. It should have been Berlin, where they dropped the A-bomb. Let the pillar of cloud and the pillar of fire appear again, like it did for Moses to lead us out of Egypt. It went before and showed the way and that's what we needed at the end of the Second World War. A way to lead us past what happened. Let the fireball come and the cloud rise above Berlin and we would follow and say, Here is the wrath of God and the retribution of God, here is God's declaration about all of the bodies of our mothers and fathers and grand-*

mothers and grandfathers and aunts and uncles and children and sisters and brothers and friends and teachers and neighbors and strangers who all were linked to us not just by blood but also by the sharing of thousands of years of history, thousands of years of trying to follow the will of God, here is God's declaration about all the brutalized and murdered bodies of all these people who are our own. Here, in this pillar of cloud and fire, these bodies are declared once and for all to be worthy of the visitation upon their abusers of the worst horror that man can make on this earth. Let Japan fall brick by brick and wound by wound, but let those who defiled this people whose nation was a shared love of God, let those monsters be vaporized in a vision that Moses himself might recognize. And this vision of fire and cloud would lead us again. It would lead us to a place where we might finally live a life free from a daily, bone-deep memory of these terrible things that happened to millions of us. I go down into the subway and I hear a cry of metal from the tunnel; I walk out of my apartment onto Tenth Street heading for a morning coffee and bagel and I see vapor rising from a manhole; I pass a brownstone and it's garbage day and a bag is torn open and I see bones, tiny bones scattered there; and I find myself living in the wilderness of history, and I want a way out, I want someone to lead me from this place to another place where the past is avenged and abandoned.

I sound like a religious man. God forbid you should take me for that. My mother and father were both lefties from the old school. They had me late—Mama was past forty—and I was their only child. For my two grandmothers I was their little shayna boychik, but for my mother and father I was their right-thinking Marxist youth. My father's father was a Bolshevik who thought Leon Trotsky was the model of what Jews would finally become in the twentieth century. The Überjuden. Not that he fared any better than his hero. He was clubbed to death by a policeman in 1937 at the Republic Steel Memorial Day Massacre, three years before Trotsky got an ax blade in the head in Mexico. My father was

*just seventeen, but he'd learned well from his father. My mother's fa-
ther was a leftist, too, a Jewish boy from Brooklyn Heights who died in
Spain fighting Franco. So this was the Tradition in my family. We never
lit a Shabbat candle, never went to temple, but we made a pilgrimage to
Highgate Cemetery in London and laid a stone on Marx's grave, and
every summer my parents sent me to a leftist summer camp up in the
Adirondacks.*

*Maybe I should have learned from my father like he learned from
his. He sorted the world out a different way. It's not if you're a Jew or
not a Jew, it's whether you're a worker or an exploiter. The camp was
full of the children of leftist Jews like my parents. But there were plenty
of others there, too. Without a God, who of course was the big capitalist
boss in the sky running the Corporation of Opiates for the Masses, if you
overthrew him, then there was no people chosen by God. Jewish meant
the same as Irish or Italian or German or English. And there were exploited working classes among all those peoples, and there were true
believers in the dialectics of history, too. This was a chosen brotherhood.*

*Which fit the times pretty well. It was the sixties when I went
every summer to camp. And we'd do craft projects on exploited peoples
of the world and skits on great moments in socialist history and at night
we'd watch films like The Grapes of Wrath and The Battleship Potemkin
and we'd sing, of course. There was plenty of singing. At lights out every
night our prepubescent voices piped out into the darkness of the
mountains: "So comrades, come rally and the last fight let us face, The
Internationale unites the human race."*

*That's what my father would have had me learn from him. He saw
Hitler's ovens as an expression of the capitalist spirit. Nazism and capitalism thrived together in Germany, they were locked in a passionate
embrace, soulmates, which I guess was true enough. "Away with all your
superstitions, servile masses arise, arise. We'll change henceforth the old
tradition." I sang with a fervor at camp to make my parents proud, and*

I suppose they were. And there were a lot of songs, not just "The Internationale." That's the first one to come to mind, with me suddenly remembering all this, but we had a leftist hymnal published by the IWW, called the Little Red Song Book, and we sang all those songs, and now that I think of it, there was another song that stood out for me back then. In 1914 the capitalist bosses of the copper mines framed a man named Joe Hill for murder because he was like a working-class troubadour wandering from migrant worker camp to hobo jungle to city slum and singing about the truths of capitalist exploitation. He died a martyr before a firing squad. Many of the songs in the Wobblies' songbook were written by Joe Hill, but one of them was written about him, after his death.

I haven't thought about all this in a very long time. That camp sat in the center of almost every year of my childhood, but there's so much that's just faded away. I grew up to disappoint my father, I suppose. I still visit him once a week in his apartment in Brooklyn and he sits at the kitchen table and spreads out the New York Times and he interprets the news for me in a steady stream of Marxist analysis and at the end he always shouts at me, "You're not hearing what I'm saying," and I say, "I'm listening, Papa. I'm listening," and he says, "Listening and hearing are two different things," and I say, "Saying and propagandizing are two different things," and it goes like this every time. We have this ritual dialectic and when I say I have to go, he gives me a handshake, but he will not look me in the eyes.

What did I know of death when I was a child? Joe Hill was shot to death. It meant nothing to me, except as an idea. The Holocaust was the same. I'd heard the tales of those things, I'd heard the numbers of the dead, I'd heard the invocation of mother and father and sister and brother, lost, gassed and incinerated. But I was a child. I knew nothing of death, except as an idea, a child's idea. I sang, "I dreamed I saw Joe Hill last night." I sang, "'The copper bosses killed you, Joe. They shot you, Joe,' says I. 'Takes more than guns to kill a man,' says Joe. 'I didn't die.' Says Joe, 'I didn't die.'" And maybe that's why the song stuck with me. Joe said he wasn't really dead. With what little I knew directly of the world, that seemed more real to me. And it took the edge off the tales of the Big Death, the millions. Joe wasn't even Jewish. If he could do it, if he could overcome death, so could they.

But then there was Tony Marcello.

I don't know what's going on in my head right now. I'd put him out of me long ago.

He was a kid from Philly, a first-timer at the camp, and he had some kind of grandfather situation, too, his father's father, I think it was, being close with Palmiro Togliatti. It was another like-grandfather-like-father thing, though on his mother's side everyone was still a practicing Catholic, praying to the saints and so forth. Tony bunked right beside me—he and I were both on the top of doubles—and I never could get to sleep too fast, even in the mountain air, and I remember every night listening to him breathe. He was louder than the crickets, though it wasn't a snore he made, exactly, the air just seemed to move heavily inside him and I could hear it and I'd listen to him, even though I didn't want to.

And it was about four weeks into the summer that one day we all went swimming in the lake. Officially, this was, with the camp counselors and all—there were a few nonpolitical summer-camp-type things we did—and Tony was a good swimmer. So he heads out deep, and this all happened so quick and simple that it just made things hit me even harder. He swims out and one of the counselors calls to him to come back. I was clinging to a post on the little wooden pier because I wasn't a good swimmer and I was scared of the water and I was just holding on there in the shadow of the pier and waiting for this to be over. But when the counselor calls out to Tony, I look and I see him maybe a hundred yards out and he stops and his head bobs up and then he goes down. I figure he's just turning around or something, or swimming back a ways under-water, which I guess is what the counselor is thinking too. But after a few moments, Tony's head comes up again and it's in just the same spot and this time it's quick, just up and back down, and the counselor jumps in and starts swimming out.

I don't know exactly how it went. Another counselor leaped in, too, and a third one took all the rest of us out of the water and brought us up to the mess hall, and this is where an atheist is at a disadvantage, I sup-pose. It was hard to apply the dialectic of history and the oppression of the working masses to what was happening in the lake. And to their credit they didn't try. They just let us be. So I started inching my way back to what I somehow knew I had to witness. I went to the mess hall door and nobody stopped me. Then I went out into the sun and over to the edge of the slope that led to the lake and nobody stopped me. There were a few people on the pier and somebody near them in the lake and then there was some activity between them and I went down the slope. I lowered my eyes and watched the rutted path as I walked but I went down to the lake and I arrived just as they laid Tony's body out on the pier. Once it was there, they sort of backed away a little, struck themselves, I guess, by the thingness of it.

And I came up to them and pushed between them and I looked at Tony Marcello, or what used to be him, because that's how I saw it, clearly. His body was laid out chest down and flat, his arms at his side, his palms up, his face turned away from me, and his death fell into my mind and then straight to the center of my own chest and into my own limbs, which suddenly were sharply aware of the tenuousness of their own animation. There was a terrible lumpenness about this body be-fore me, a heaviness, an absence. Tony Marcello was gone. Gone and done with. And all of a sudden, from the body of this boy who was no Jew at all, far from it, from the body of this boy who was a Christian,

at least by the prayers of his mama and his mama's mama, from the
body of this boy, I finally felt the thing that happened to all those Jews
as real.

    So I guess I didn't put Tony Marcello out of me at all. He turned
into a cry in a subway tunnel, a puff of vapor from a manhole, a scatter-
ing of bones on a sidewalk. And I really did dream of Joe Hill. For weeks
after that, every night, I'd wake in my bunk bed and there must have
been the sounds of other boys sleeping all around me and the chirr of
crickets outside but all I'd hear was this silence, this clear and deafening
absence of Tony Marcello's breath, and I'd be in a cold sweat and I knew
I'd been dreaming of Joe Hill. He stood on a pier by a lake and they shot
him dead and he fell in the water and disappeared without a trace, and
I knew he was gone and I knew he was dead, no matter what he said, he
was dead. And in my dream, he was a Jew.

    And Jacob Klein dreamed again. His words stopped and he
dreamed and I was afraid of his dreams. I am afraid once more. Of
Arthur's dreams, of Viola's dreams, of Judith Marie Nash's dreams,
of my wife Edna Bradshaw's dreams, of the dreams of all those
creatures there below. I am afraid. For them and for myself. They
live so intensely with such difficult desiderata. And I Think I'm
Going Out of My Head. It is not Jacob Klein before me. He has
returned to his life down there, his memory of me gone forever,
like Tony Marcello. This is one thing that has brought on this spasm
of fear, I realize. I am Tony Marcello to hundreds on this planet. I
am before them, I am even part of them, I share their voices, and
then I am gone forever. Worse. Tony Marcello's body was gone
and yet Jacob Klein kept a memory of him. I am gone from these
lives and nothing of me remains. Nothing. Except with Edna
Bradshaw. And with Minnie Butterworth, whom I allowed to remember. Does she think of me still? But no. Now it is she who is
dead. Almost certainly dead. But I am not. I am not. Though I am

in no one's dreams on this planet, I am still alive. How fuzzy in my thinking I have become. How self-absorbed. I turned to Jacob Klein's voice seeking the third red white and blue eagle and the big jackpot of understanding, I would know this species at last, not in my own terms but in theirs, but I cannot put these three voices together, I am losing the meaning of even any one of them. I have only blanks before me.

I look at Arthur sleeping. His fingers move slightly. He touches someone in his dream, perhaps. I am reminded of Eddie the yellow cat. When he sleeps, his paws sometimes move, faintly, as if he is running. His toes flare and his claws come out. He dreams. He chases other subspecies creatures in his dreams to grab them and kill them and eat them. Perhaps the place where dreams come from is impervious to my power to bring forgetfulness. Perhaps they have all dreamed of me, all these visitors from Earth. Who is to say? Perhaps they chase me and grab me and kill me in their dreams.

I am growing quite hysterical, am I not? But, of course, I am very tired. Very tired. And this planet spins on, pulling the end of its millennium toward it. Only a few hours away, and I have no plan for what I must do. I think to wake Arthur now and return him to his sleeping place. I see myself doing this very thing, though I am aware that I have not moved at all from my chair. This is merely my intention for the next few minutes playing itself out in my mind. But no. I am actually doing this thing. Surely I am. I rise and touch Arthur on the arm and he snaps awake and looks up at me.

"It is time," I say.

"Have you come to take me home?" Arthur asks.

"Only to the place on my ship where you sleep," I say.

He reaches up and grasps my arm. "Am I in heaven?"

"You are not dead."

"Aren't you the Lord?"

"Am I?"

"Yes. You've come to take me."

"How do you know?" I say.

"We have been waiting for you. Forever."

"Please," I say. "Come now. Sleep."

And Arthur falls from the chair to his knees and bends low before me. "Lord," he says. "I will rest in you."

"Only your voice will. I am sorry. I wish it were more."

And now the door to the interview room opens with a great whoosh of air and with a flood of light from the corridor and I turn and there are silhouettes there, one and then another and they are sliding into the room, another silhouette enters and another, and they are simply dark, sharply outlined shapes, and there are more coming in and they gather around me now and the lights catch them, there are so many of these creatures that all the lights of the room flare up at once and it is very bright, and they are the rest of my twelve, my Viola and my Lucky and my Mary and my Hank and my Trey and my Hudson and my Claudia and my Digger and my Misty and my Jared and now my Citrus, who breaks through all of them and she has wiped the blackness from her mouth and her lips are pale, the color of my wife Edna Bradshaw's thighs, and the black spikes of Citrus's hair have dissolved into long silken curls of russet which fall about her shoulders and the metal piercings are gone from her face and all of these voices cry out, "Lord, Lord what will you have us do?"

And I cry, "I am."

And I wait. And I look at these twelve faces hovering before me and I feel these twelve minds waiting for more. And I think, Surely that is what this world needs to understand. It is the fundamental truth I have to speak. From that truth all things will follow for each of them. But they wait, they do not respond, the faces hover blankly.

Then Hudson says, "You am what?"

And they all say, "You am what?"

And I say, "I am that I am."

And Hudson says, "What the fuck does that mean?"

And they all say, "What the fuck does that mean?"

And I try to shape some further revelation. I am thinking to say, I am a spaceman. I am a sharer of your voices. I am one who yearns and grieves with you.

But before I can speak, Citrus says, "He am God!"

"God!" they all cry and their faces fall, clustering together now low to the floor at the edge of the light, and from them, Citrus's voice rises.

She says, "He has spoken the words of God to Moses at Horeb. He is God!"

"I am not!" I say, though my voice sounds faint to me.

"Do not forsake us!" Citrus cries.

And they all cry, "Do not forsake us!"

And I say, "Go to sleep."

And Claudia says, "Sleep! He wants us to die!"

Claudia's voice is full of fear and I am afraid she will draw her pistol again. I cry out loud and sharp, "Sleep! Merely sleep!"

And Arthur's voice rises now, "He says there's nothing after death!"

And Hudson cries. "Merely sleep! We're in deep!"

A great wave of moans sweeps across all of them.

Citrus's face rises from the gathering near the floor. Her eyes are full of tears. "Are those the words you haven't been saying to me?"

"No." I cannot make my voice rise above a whisper.

The tears are rushing down Citrus's face now and down the faces of the others, too, for they are all weeping copiously, and Citrus says, "Why are you forsaking us?"

"I do not wish to forsake you," I say, and I lift my hands, I will try to touch them, I will place the beating of my heart inside each of them. But as soon as my hands appear, they all recoil.

Hank the bus driver's voice lifts sharply, "That's how he makes us sleep!"

And others cry, "The hands!"

And Citrus emerges into the light, her whole body, clothed in the whiteness of a nuclear fireball, and she lifts her hands even as mine still rise from the momentum of my impulse to help these yearning souls and in each of her hands is a glint of light in each of her hands is a long tapering shape in each of her hands is a metal spike and I wish to cry out but there is nothing to say and Citrus's hands rear back and her face is twisted in pain and I see the flash of spikes as they rush at *my* hands, spikes Sharp Enough to Cut Tin Cans Sharp Enough for All Your Kitchen Needs, and I cannot hide my hands, I cannot move my hands at all, and my palms suddenly burn as if the very atoms that make them up are flying apart and I am about to flare into nothingness.

And I leap up. I am aflame and I am stiff but I am standing alone in my interview room. I spin to face the door and it is in darkness, closed tight. I am alone.

No. Not alone. I sense another, and I turn, slowly, and look.

It is Arthur. He sleeps, still, in his chair.

I look again toward the door and then into the places where the others had been. There is no one. They have vanished.

Or they were never there.

And suddenly I realize that I have dreamed.

My species does not dream. I have only music inside me when I sleep. It is mere sleep. But now I have dreamed. I have died my daily death and instead of darkness and an ineffable movement of tone, I have voices and faces and the anguish of others, and my own anguish as well, a terrible burning. I look at my hands. They are unharmed. But that merely preserves them for further harm when next I fall asleep. I have died my daily death and descended into the hell of dreams.

13

I lie down beside my wife Edna Bradshaw, where she sleeps within the covers of our bed. I listen to the sound she makes, and though she is not snoring, the air seems to move heavily inside her and I can hear it clearly and she is louder than the crickets in the Adirondack Mountains. Though I have never personally heard the crickets in the Adirondack Mountains, I am sure that this is true about my wife's breathing. And it frightens me, of course, for I fear that she will swim out too far and she will drown. An unreasonable fear. She is safe on my spaceship. She will never have occasion to swim in a lake in the Adirondacks. My fear abates. But now I am sad, for I myself will never hear the chirring of the crickets in the Adirondacks, or in any mountains. Or perhaps I will. Perhaps I will descend from my spaceship in less than twenty hours—I checked the time again after my dream—and the world will welcome the truth that I exist and they will embrace me and slap me on the back in gestures of acceptance and affection, I will be their pardner, and they will say: Go, see, listen, let it all hang out, do your thing, the world is your oyster, wash the dirt right down your drain, fish in our streams, hunt in our woods, swim in our lakes. And I grow frightened again.

I draw near to my wife. I am glad for the prominent sound of her breath. I bring my face next to hers, I let the exhalation of her breath touch my eyes. I reach up and take her face gently in my hands, touching her with my fingertips, exchanging heartbeats for breaths. And she says, softly, "Oh you spaceman."

"I am sorry I awoke you," I say, not moving my hands.

"Oh you go ahead and wake me like this any old time," she says.

Regrettably I cannot shape the *words* this world demands of its creatures without ceasing the sharing of my heart, and so I take my hands away from her face.

She sighs.

I say, "May I ask you two questions?"

"Of course, honey," she says.

"When you dream, do you dream of Desi your spaceman husband?"

She rises up now from beneath the covers, throwing them off as if she were emerging from deep water in a dazzling rebirth, for though, when I laid her down to sleep at the beginning of this long night, I had simply helped her—sleepy bunny that she was—into her pink fuzzy wuzzies, now she flares and sparkles in the light in her Glittery Gold Harem Dazzler. "You mean Desi my husband *and* my spaceman lover?" she says, adjusting herself within her Shaped Sequin Bra.

"Yes," I say, though the word goes mushy, formed as it is by my suddenly floppy tongue. "I remain your spaceman lover as well."

"Of course I dream of you."

"Why of course?"

She smiles and giggles and moves her hand as if she will pinch my cheek. I cannot face this gesture of affection tonight and so I withdraw from her reach, trying to mask my retreat as an intention to sit up and square around to face her. I think of my own dream, how my visitors all recoiled at the lifting of my hands.

"Girls always dream about their beaus," Edna says.

"I am in retreat in your dreams," I say. "I start as your husband and then I am your lover—am I not correct in thinking that, strictly speaking, this role, though similar in activity, is subsumed in the role of husband?—and now I am your beau, which is your boyfriend before becoming your lover. Do I misunderstand these words?"

Edna stops and thinks about this for a long moment. "You know, I hadn't thought about it, but you're right. Now sometimes a girl will say *beau* when she means lover, if she's in polite company or if she's with her girlfriends at the hairdressers or somewhere and they can all have fun winking at each other and making little we-know-what-you're-really-saying sounds, because it's like a secret code between you. And, of course, it's a sad thing but true that most *husbands* don't keep doing the basic activity you pretty much always have with a *lover*. But still, you're right. A beau transforms into a lover and then into a husband, like a worm turning by stages into a butterfly. Except most times it's more like a butterfly of a beau transforming into a worm of husband. But you do listen real good, don't you my honeybun. Now *there's* something that husband, lover, *and* beau all three most often are real neglectful at. A girl does like to be listened to, especially if she loves to talk, which I do, though you probably already know that."

And Edna stops talking abruptly. Her brow knits and then her face does a quick turn slightly to the left as if she has just seen the darting of some tiny animal on the floor, and then her face does a similar quick turn to the right. "Where was I?" she asks.

"Loving to talk," I say.

"Before that."

"Dreams," I say.

"I think it's true," she says. "I think a girl dreams of her beau more than her lover and her lover more than her husband. Probably a lot more. You dream about the things you want."

"And the dreams that frighten you?"

"You also dream about things that frighten you, it's true. But it's not so different. It's still about wanting. You want to escape those things. You run in your dreams, you scream, you weep. You want it to end."

"But aren't there sweet dreams?"

"There's some that are sweet enough while you're in them, but you wake up and they're gone. That loving handsome man's not there in the bed beside you. You didn't actually make a speech on the Fourth of July to all of Bovary and they cheered for you. You can't really flap your arms and fly high along the Pigeon River. You're left with a whole lot of wanting again."

I say, "I am not surprised at what you say. I have made a mistake to link the thing I wish for to dreams. What I wish for is to be in your memory. It can be in memories of your waking state, as well. I wish to be always inside you."

Edna Bradshaw leans forward and puts her hand on mine. Her bazongas—I can only think of them as that, held, as they are, by these besequined cups of gold—her bazongas surge and pucker at their place of cleavage. Sweet dreams are made of these. And she says, "You're always inside me, you spaceman lover you. You're the proof that dreams come true."

In spite of the billowing of my wife Edna Bradshaw's bazongas, and though I have had only one dream in my life, I am struck with fear at this notion.

I wish to stop speaking now. I need to sleep. But the fear that sprung from dreams and again from the thought of dreams fulfilled now leaps back into me at the prospect of falling asleep. I am a member of my own species but I have taken on the nature of this species. I am as vulnerable as they.

"Didn't you say you had two questions?"

I look at my wife Edna Bradshaw, who has just spoken to me. I struggle to comprehend the words. She seems to understand my difficulty.

"Two questions," she says. "You said you had two."

"Yes," I say. "What is a roller rink?"

"You do have such an interesting mind, Desi honey. Going from one thing to another. Well, a roller rink—and we do have one in Bovary, Alabama, though I never mention it when I say to people what there is to do in town, I always just say the Rebel Roll Bowling Alley and Sam's Skeet Shoot and, of course, people like to hang out at the Dairy Freeze, and that's all I say, even though the Dixie-Do Roller Rink sits not a quarter of a mile from the Wal-Mart where you and I met—a roller rink, on the one hand, is a place with a big hardwood floor and flashing colored lights where people strap wheels on their feet and roll around to fast music, but on the other hand, it's a place where you choose to go if you're a girl who wants to humiliate herself before the whole world in numerous ways, like having to call out your shoe size in front of everybody when you've got a size-ten foot and you even are fool enough to ask for double-E width and they laugh and give you about a size-six set of roller skates and say to squeeze into these honey and then you go on to try to follow every little activity the DJ, who's the guy running the music, gives you, from Presto Chango, where you have to suddenly change direction, to Backwards Time, where everybody has to skate backwards, to the Hokey Pokey, where you gather around and you extend various parts of your body into the circle and shake them all about, all of which activities are designed to make you fall down, which I always did with a great flopping and trembling of my then too ample flesh, if you know what I mean. That's a roller rink. Hell on wheels."

"I am sorry," I say.

"What in heaven's name for?"

"I made you remember the place that humiliated you."

"The Dixie-Do Roller Rink? Oh don't you be worrying your sweet spaceman head. That old life is dead and gone. But people can be pretty cruel sometimes. . . . Where are you going?"

I have jumped up from the bed, full of anxiety. It is the capacity for cruelty in these creatures that I fear. I say, "There is so little time left."

"For what?"

This is a question I do not feel prepared to answer. Though I should. By tomorrow all the planet will know. And this is my wife before me. There is nothing in my directive that would prohibit letting my wife know my mission, especially this near to the hour and in the safe confines of our spaceship. But I am not yet prepared to shape these words of explanation. I am frightened.

"Desi honey, what is it? What's wrong?"

"Nothing is wrong, my dear wife Edna Bradshaw," I say.

"I thought we'd pretty much cured you of addressing me in that formal spaceman way. Something *is* bothering you."

"I have a task." I find I can say no more.

Edna waits a few moments and then tries to fill in the blank I have left. "You're a hardworking man, I know that."

"I am a hardworking man. This is true. I am an okay Joe. I am a friendly guy. There is nothing to be afraid of. I come in peace, Earthlings."

"What are you going on about?"

"You have nothing to fear," I say.

"Then why does your saying that scare me?"

"Why does your being scared of me scare me?" I cry. All of this is going very badly.

And my wife cries in return, "I don't know why me being scared of you saying not to be scared scares you, but that scares me even more."

This answer is clear to me. "Because if I scare you by asking you not to be scared—you who are my wife Edna Bradshaw who loves me—then how scared will all the creatures on this planet be when I obey my orders to descend from my spaceship and reveal the existence of spacemen to the whole world?"

And now it has been spoken between us.

Edna lowers herself to the bed. She sits and she is, for the moment, uncharacteristically, speechless.

I begin to hum. But at the first sound of this, Edna's face turns to me and she is wide-eyed with fear and I stop.

"I am sorry," I say. "Whenever I Feel Afraid, I Whistle a Happy Tune."

"That was no whistle," Edna says, softly.

"A spaceman whistle," I say.

"They'll tear you apart down there," she says.

"What Do Doctors Do To Relieve Tense Nervous Headaches?" I say.

"This is no time for that kind of talk, Desi honey. Turn off that TV in your head."

Unexpectedly, I find that her words Make My Brown Eyes Blue. I sit down beside her.

"I've gone and hurt your feelings," she says.

"Did you read my mind?" I cry, full of hope.

"I read your face, honeybun. When your feelings are hurt, that wide sweet mouth of yours wrinkles up like a Mary-Lou's-Southern-Belle-Beauty-Nook marcel wave. Like now."

"What is wrong with the TV in my head?"

"There's a lot of good things on TV. I'm not saying there's not. You're full of tasty tidbits from your listening in and all. But this is the real world you're about to face."

My wife Edna Bradshaw is confirming my worst fears now. There is the world I have learned about all these years and then there is a *real* world that has eluded me all along. I know nothing.

Her eyes widen. "Now I've never seen your mouth do *that,* honey. Like it was a lie-detecting machine and I just told the biggest whopper ever. I don't mean to keep on hurting your feelings. But the truth is I'm scared for you."

I say, "I am scared too."

"I don't ever interfere with my man's work. That's not what's done where I come from. But please, Desi, can't we just go off to some other world now? Let's try a new place. Listen in on Mars or somewhere."

"There are only rocks on Mars."

Edna bends near to me. She places her hand on mine. "Anywhere," she says. "Please."

"I am," I say, "who I am."

My wife Edna Bradshaw thinks about this for a moment and then she says in a voice that is very soft and with her eyes filling with the tears that still seem so alien to me. "Yes you are," she says. "And I would not want that any other way."

I say, "Time has run out for me, Edna Bradshaw my honeybun. I go down to your planet tonight at midnight. But I am very tired. I must rest. And yet I must talk with more of our guests. Are they not from the real world you speak of? Perhaps I can still learn."

"Has it done you any good so far, all your interviewing?" she asks.

"I thought yes, for a long while, yes, at least to some extent, but now I am not so sure. Still, I must try. I must listen. I must learn. I . . . yearn for these things, my wife Edna Bradshaw. That is the word for what I do. Like all of you. I yearn. To seek. To know."

"Do you also yearn to go down there and tell all those folks who are so full of themselves and have so many ways to hurt one another that they ain't such big fish in the universe after all? Ida Mae Pickett, my best friend in the world for many years, she yearned once, too, she even said that word one day in the beauty parlor and I didn't trust it in her mouth, not for one second. She yearned to go off to Montgomery, she said, and make a name for herself doing the hair of capital hostesses and lady lawyers and people like that and maybe even the hair of the wife of the governor of the great state of Alabama someday. And Ida Mae was back in Bovary in no time and she wasn't talking about Montgomery—rather not say a thing, thank you very much for not asking—and it was plain to see she'd been yearning for the wrong things and found nothing but grief for herself. Don't talk to me about *yearning.* Better you should just *want* a few things. You might can get something you *want.* But nobody ever gets a yearning, I bet. That just goes on and on."

"Do you have only *wants,* my wife Edna Bradshaw?"

"I try."

"But then is it not true that you yearn not to yearn?"

My wife flutters her hands and she looks here and there about the room. Clunkheadedly, I have made her uncomfortable. "I am sorry," I say. "It is just a word. I have always scorned these bits of sound on this planet and here I am, pursuing my wife to a state of discomfy with a word. A word I think far too much about. Perhaps I am not in the real world now. Though I have never heard the word in question in the heightened discourse that has so interested me in the *unreal* world. Oh oh, I yearn for Spaghet-

tios! I yearn for a Twinkie! I yearn for TwoAllBeefPattiesSpecial-
SauceLettuceCheesePicklesOnionsOnA SesameSeedBun! I yearn
for the Breakfast of Champions! No! *These* are 'wants.' And yes,
you are right, my wife Edna Bradshaw. I can have any one of them.
So can you. So can anyone. It is simple! It is economical! It is
America! I want! I want! I am my wants. I can have my wants. I
can be me! I gotta be me!"

I find myself standing on the bed, straight and proud, my wife
Edna Bradshaw's face turned up to me in wonder. We consider
each other for a long moment.

Then my wife says, "Desi? Are you all right, honey? What do
you want right now?"

"I want what I cannot have. More time. I want to listen to our
guests."

"I can fix that, honeybun. Please. Sit down."

And I do. I sit before my wife, my mate, my spouse, my old
lady, my better half, my helpmeet. Though my mind is careening
on. I sit.

Edna Bradshaw says, "We should have a nice fancy sit-down
supper for everybody. You can talk with them all and you can see
how they are together."

I grow floppy with appreciation at my wife. "This is a very
good idea," I say. "But there is so little time."

"Have you forgotten who you're married to, Mr. Spaceman?
I'll have things ready in plenty of time. It's only right, anyway. You
wouldn't want our guests to sleep through this special New Year's
Eve." And the wife I clearly remember marrying, Edna Louise
Bradshaw, bounces off the bed. "If the dinner's a big success maybe
you won't have to go down there after all."

I do not have the heart to argue this point with her. Perhaps
her want has turned into a yearning. Not that creatures on this

planet—or any planet in the universe—can get even all their *wants,* either. But I want to obey the powers that sent me to this world, even if I do not want to do the thing they ask of me. And I must obey. But I do not speak these thoughts to my wife, and at this moment I am grateful for the barrier between our minds.

"My mind is on the job already," she says. "Don't ask. Don't ask. It'll be a surprise. You're in the hands of an expert at this, if I do say so myself—and I just did—though I hope you won't think I'm being too prideful. But you do have a choice to make. It must be chicken. Without knowing anything else about this mixed group we have here, you can go wrong with all other main dishes except chicken. Chicken is safe. That's not the choice I refer to. I just want you to consider two things right now, however, Desi. Chicken Lickin'. Or Chicken Wiggle."

She pauses as if the salient qualities of these two things are already apparent to me. Since her earlier observations about my physiology, I find myself inordinately conscious of my mouth. It has drawn tight, I think. Edna observes this.

"Silly me," she says. "Chicken Wiggle. We're talking boiled chicken cut into chunks. Onions, canned English peas, Worcester-shire sauce, pimento, mushroom soup, chopped bell peppers, a dash of Tabasco. All mixed with egg noodles. And then with Chicken Lickin' it's baked whole chicken dipped in milk and creamy peanut butter with paprika and Accent and . . . wait a minute." Edna slaps her own forehead. "Stop right there. We don't know if anybody has a peanut allergy. That can kill you dead."

She looks at me. I am still stuck on boiled and cut and baked chickens. Perfectly innocent birds, it seems to me. Perhaps with their own feelings and their own language rivaling Eddie the yel-low cat's in complexity. My wife would never consider boiling, cutting, and baking Eddie.

"So it's Chicken Wiggle," Edna says. "That settles it. I may have to get you to beam me up some Worcestershire sauce, but I think I've stocked up on everything else."

And she disappears into the bathroom to dress. I can hear her whistling.

"That is a happy tune," I say.

"It's 'Dixie,'" she calls from the bathroom. "Happy and sad, really."

"Happy and sad," I repeat, but low, only for myself. There is a sound of water running now. I wish there were a chicken before me, to apologize to. But that is not the true issue, I realize. The sad things are complex, too complex for me to deal with at this moment. And yet, I am happy at the wonderful plan that my wife Edna Bradshaw has presented to me. We will have a nice big supper before I descend to the planet Earth. If it is a success, I will know what to do, what to say when I go down there. I will ask all my guests to put their heads together to help me.

I feel bloated with weariness. I am so weary I cannot even hear the music of sleep beginning to shape in me. I am that weary. And it is all right now, to sleep. Edna will wake me for the supper and until then I can sleep. Still, something in me wants to hear another voice. It is not so easy to abandon the pattern of my professional life, no matter how weary I am. And I am weary. I should sleep. I should sleep but I rise up from the bed and I go to the door that leads into the corridor and before I move to open it I can feel that there is someone on the other side. I know this as surely as if a member of my own species were standing there, waiting, placing his presence in my head, placing his consciousness there. *Her* presence. I realize there is a female on the other side of the door. I imagine that it might indeed be a member of my own species. A supervisor come to give me last-minute instructions or to fortify my courage.

I move my hand.

The door opens.

And it is Claudia.

I look instantly to her hands, though I know I have her weapon in my Hall of Objects. But I also had her in her sleeping space, unconscious. Anything is possible. But she simply opens her empty hands before me.

"I've been waiting a long time to speak with you," she says. "Please."

"I was just coming to get you," I say, and that certainly could be true. I was in fact going to get *someone* and she is a legitimate choice.

At this, Claudia turns on her heel and moves off down the corridor. I follow. She goes straight to the interview room and the door opens for her and by the time I step in, she is sitting in the appropriate chair, a shaft of light illuminating her.

I sit before her. She closes her eyes and without my even having to wave my hand her voice starts and mine starts with hers and we speak and I am Claudia Lambert. *I feel like I should give you a formal welcome. I worked for NASA for nearly a decade. But other things overtook me. I worked for NASA but now I work for myself with my name on the door and a payroll of a dozen and nobody above me who I can turn to for appreciation. I had a daughter but now I have a twenty-one-year-old friend, such a good friend that she can tell me only the truth when I'm being stupid or a fool. I had faith in the institutions of the city of Houston and the state of Texas but now I carry a pistol in my purse, since concealed weapons in Texas are suddenly legal and I'm afraid of accidentally cutting somebody off on the interstate and them taking out a gun and trying to shoot me. I'll be able to shoot back at them. Road rage enrages me. I hate the instant and harsh criticism of drivers trying to feel self-righteous over petty little things and I feel self-righteous hating them. I had a husband but now my body is my own and I can't find anybody I'd even want to hold hands with after an hour's conversation much less choose to take to bed.*

God I loved the space program. Especially the two Voyagers. I love the Voyagers even more now, I think. They're carrying these electronic records of who we are, the people of Earth. They'll carry them for millennia and millennia, out into the stars. Not that I ever bought the hodgepodge image they've got of us. But it's something. Among the music selections, they've got the first movement of Beethoven's Fifth flying out there and right alongside is Chuck Berry doing "Johnny B. Goode." There's an image of a traffic jam in India next to a tree toad next to a demonstration of human sex organs. And there's fifty-five different speakers in fifty-five languages giving greetings. Mostly, Hello from earth. Peace to you. That sort of thing. But each one's a little different. The Zulu speaking Nguni calls the spacemen "great ones" and wishes them longevity. The Turk co-opts them right away, addressing them as "Turkish-speaking friends." The Indonesian seems to be the host of a TV talk show. He says, "Good night, ladies and gentlemen. Good-bye and see you next time." And the young woman doing the Swedish refused to step out of the bounds of her own little life. She says, "Greetings from a computer programmer in the little university town of Ithaca on the planet Earth." What are the spacemen going to think? Ithaca's in Sweden, I guess. I don't know why I should give a damn. I can't send a verbal greeting that can be adequately comprehended across a lunch table in River Oaks to my own daughter once a week.

But I did know how to turn NASA technical stuff into ideas and images the press could understand. And I did that for a while. Even now when I think about my life, it's all Voyager 2. I got married the day it took off. When it was between the Earth and the asteroid belt I was happy. Jenny was born two weeks from Jupiter. Between Jupiter and Saturn I got divorced. Flying by Saturn, I went to work for NASA, and between Saturn and Uranus I thought I was happy again, buried in my work. Between Uranus and Neptune I wanted to get the hell away from people, from bosses, and just take care of myself and my baby and it still took a while. It wasn't until after Neptune. It wasn't until Voyager 2 suddenly was looking ahead and all that was out there was forty thousand years to the nearest star, it wasn't until then that I could walk away. But I had a marketable skill for high-tech companies in Houston and elsewhere. I was somebody who could explain things like heliopause, which is what the scientists expect Voyager will locate for them sometime around the turn of the millennium. It's the outermost boundary of the solar wind, which is made up of charged atomic particles sheering off from the Sun as it drags us all through space. At the heliopause the solar wind gets hemmed in by all the charged particles floating around in interstellar space. It puts the whole solar system in a big magnetic bubble. And so I whipped on past NASA, getting a big acceleration from its gravity, like Voyager accelerating past Neptune, and I was out on my own, with a lot of empty space ahead.

But that's been more than ten years and now my little girl sits across from me over her spinach salad with sprouts and she's a young woman and she tells me, "Mama why are you so militant? Men aren't so bad. So they're, like, from their own planet. That's okay. But I'm afraid you've left Venus and moved to Mars." And I have no idea where she got the capacity to absorb shit ideas like that.

But I guess I'm still looking for something to put in the center of me, where all the shit ideas once were. I can sit in my office for hours, after everyone else has gone home, and my office is dark and the shades are open to the night sky. I can sit there and think about how it was supposed to go for a woman's life on this planet, for centuries—you must *subordinate yourself; you are your devotion to your man; you find your excellence in the role the world gives you—and of course I understand how all that separated women from a chance to find their personal destinies. But I keep coming around to this. At the end of the day, the things the men tried to keep for themselves—you are your work; you are born to conquer and dominate; you make your own fate, find your own excellence—these things leave the even bigger questions unanswered, too. Just as badly. The questions that your job, your children, your marriage, your ideas, your personal destiny on this lump of cosmic rock just won't get at. Not with the downright infinity of things hovering over you in the dark every night. But then I think about our little Voyager out there and for a moment I'm okay. Someday soon, Voyager's going to reach the heliopause. And then it'll pop out of that bubble we're all in and it'll just keep on going. Free at last. With the big mysteries ahead of it and all the time in the universe to figure them out.*

Claudia falls silent and I am instantly buoyed by her words. This thing I must do in a few hours: it will bring an answer to one of the big mysteries. Surely all those who yearn as Claudia does will welcome me. Surely the Swedish-speaking computer programmer in Ithaca would welcome me. And the Zulu, who wishes me longevity. And the Indonesian who hopes he will see me next time.

"Surely they will welcome me," I say to Claudia.

But she shakes her head sadly. No. "They're coming for you," she says.

And suddenly the light on her face begins to thrash and her eyes shift to look over my shoulder and I turn and the doorway is crowded with large men in ragged clothes and they have wild eyes and they are carrying torches alive with fire and pitchforks and the only reason they have not already burst in and grabbed me is that there are so many of them trying to squeeze through at once and I leap up and the room is silent and I turn back to Claudia but there is only an empty bed. The bed where, until this moment, I must have been sleeping. How could I? I have heard Claudia Lambert's voice so clearly.

I rush out of this space where my body seems to be. Perhaps *this* is the dream. Perhaps I have dozed off before Claudia. The dream began with the sad shake of her head. The men in the door-way: *that* is the stuff of my dream. I skim down the corridor and into the interview room.

It is empty. But it would be, if this is the dream. Still, I glide to the machine. I move my hand. I seek the voice of Claudia Lambert recorded on Earthtime December 31, 2000. She is not here. There is no record. But she wouldn't be. There is no reason for the dream machine's records to correspond with the real machine's. But why am I not waking? I stomp about the room now, moving my feet and legs like the Earthlings. I stomp and my feet flare with pain and my jaw vibrates from the blows.

I am already awake. In the empty interview room. I turn to my machine. I try once more to retrieve Claudia's voice. It is not there. She was a dream.

My next move is clear. I go out into the corridor and down to the place where my visitors are sleeping. I go in to Claudia's room and I find her there. I bend near her. I move my hand. She opens her eyes and turns her face to me.

She says, very softly, "Have you come for me?"

"Yes," I say.

"Do I vaguely remember shooting my pistol?"

"Yes. But you did not hurt anyone."

"I don't know what came over me. I'm sorry." She sits up now and wobbles a bit. I touch her shoulder to steady her.

"You will be fine in a moment," I say.

"Really. The irony is that I'm happy to be here," she says. "In spite of the impression I gave. Now that I know . . ."

"Yes. Yes," I say, and I find that I am beginning to flush hot inside and I do not know why, exactly.

And we go, Claudia and I, down the corridor, and she is very gracious and curious and friendly and I grow more and more agitated.

And now she is sitting before me in the interview room and she says, "What should I do?"

"Just relax," I say, and I move my hand.

In the brief moment before we begin to speak together I realize the source of my agitation. I am afraid of the power of my dreams. And I am Claudia Lambert. And I say, *I feel like I should give you a formal welcome. . . .*

14

And so together, swept along by the solar wind of Claudia's life, we spoke the words I had dreamed, precisely, she and I together, the very same words. She gave her Earth-voice to the yearning for answers to the big mysteries and now she falls silent, and I should not be afraid of my prophecy, I should perhaps try to understand it as a reading of Claudia's mind, not unlike the exchange of thoughts between members of my own species, effected here only in this state of dreams. But I am, nevertheless, afraid. This was a different thing. I have become a different being. Different from my own species. But different, too, from the primary species of Earth. And I am afraid the prophecy may continue to be fulfilled. Are there men with torches and pitchforks just outside the door waiting for me to speak my hope for a welcome on Earth, as I had in my dream? I keep my mouth shut. In spite of the fifty-five greetings carried on Voyager, I cannot expect a cheery hello tonight.

Claudia is looking at me, intently. "Looking into your eyes, I feel like I'm dreaming," she says.

"Did you not believe . . . ?"

"In you? That you existed? Yes."

"This is not a dream," I say, and Claudia looks over my shoulder, but I think I suddenly recognize the heliopause, that boundary between my spaceman's life and this other state, and I have just popped out of the bubble and I am heading into the vast interstellar darkness of dreams. I try to stop. I press my eyes open wide. I move my hand before my own face.

"You look tired," Claudia says. She is focused only on me. I am awake once more.

"I am very tired," I say.

"Can we speak again?" she asks.

"There will be a supper tonight, as the moment of the millennium approaches. My wife Edna Bradshaw is cooking even now. We can speak then."

Claudia leans forward, her hand coming out to me. Yes, Claudia Lambert, you may have the beating of my heart. You have sought it and you shall have it. I take her hands in mine.

She watches this entwining, conscious, I am sure, of the thing I am giving her. I say, "I am glad that after our hour of conversation you want to hold hands."

She looks at me. "Yes," she says. "Thank you."

And I escort her back to her space and she accepts my suggestion of rest. I pass my hand over her and I am unsteady on my feet and I glide away, into the corridor and back to my bed, and I am full of trepidation. I must sleep. This will be my first formal seeking of the state since I have begun to dream. I wonder if the formality of this will alter the dreams.

I pull back the covers and I wish that my wife Edna Bradshaw were lying down beside me, but she has prepared a way for me, even as I pull the covers up to my chinny-chin-chin. Now I lay me down to sleep I pray the Lord my soul to keep if I should die before I wake . . . Rockaby baby on the treetop when the wind blows the cradle will rock when the bough breaks the cradle will fall . . . It is no wonder that the children of Earth learn to dream. They sing of death, over and over, before they sleep. They die. They fall. I hear the solar wind outside the window. I hear the soft pad of

Eddie's feet across the floor. And Dick Clark stands before me. I have never interviewed Dick Clark, but for many years I have watched him, we have all watched him, when there were others of my species on the spaceship, and we all admired Dick Clark as he emceed the latest in popular music and moved his hand over a large room and people danced and danced before him and we would, too, we spacemen, we would do the twist and the stroll and later the frug and the mashed potato, though we knew that we were pitifully inadequate, floating instead of strolling, gliding instead of mashed potatoing, but Dick Clark and all his Earth Angels, all his Teenagers in Love, who danced for him taught us many things about this world while we hovered far above, imitating the steps, knowing, however, that we were Only the Lonely, and now he is dressed in his stylish blue parka jacket and his hair is carefully coiffed around his headset and he holds a microphone and it is night and beyond him is Times Square in New York City and there is a steady roar behind his characteristically sweet and reassuring and happy words, a roar like the noise from deep space, and it is the crowd, a million strong, two million, on this special New Year's Eve, and he draws our attention to the lighted ball on the tower at One Times Square and he explains it will descend and he turns to look over his shoulder and suddenly Dick Clark says, "Holy shit."

And I recognize my spaceship. It is hovering over the tower.

At first glance the ball has begun to descend, but no, Dick Clark's deep-rooted reportorial skills have been activated and he is announcing to the world this most extraordinary story.

"Ladies and gentlemen and young people everywhere," he says into his microphone, "this is not the traditional ball descending the tower at One Times Square. Instead, a circular craft, clearly of extraterrestrial origin, has appeared and is hovering over the tower. What we see, illuminated by some unearthly unknown source, is what appears to be a spaceman. He is descending slowly from the spaceship. The whole of Times Square has seen him now. A great hush has come over the massive crowd. Listen."

And Dick Clark points his microphone out in the direction of the crowd and he is right, the roar has ceased, there is only silence coming from the millions as they watch this figure descend from the machine.

Only I recognize the figure. I am. I am the figure ablaze there in light, moving before the tower—in precise time with the count-down to the millennium, as a matter of fact, which does not escape the notice of Dick Clark, who is announcing like he has never announced before, he is in the zone, in the flow, this is the zenith of his career—well, perhaps his first introduction of Chuck Berry, whose voice even now is flying out to the stars, representing the planet Earth to all the rest of us, perhaps that was a comparable moment for him—but this is a big scoop, off the entertainment pages, top of the news, and Dick knows it. He says, "This space-man is actually counting in the new millennium for us—five, four . . ."

And the crowd picks up the count, and at "three" there are a million voices and by "two" there are a million more, and it is as if they have all accepted me, I am the lighted ball, I am the next thousand years.

"One," Dick and the millions cry, and then there is a deafening cheer and an explosion of color overhead and it seems as if everyone in this vast crowd is waving at me, and I continue to descend, past the tower, past the upper floors of One Times Square, past the running electronic headlines, which already are picking up on Dick Clark's scoop: HAPPY NEW YEAR. SPACE-MAN LANDS IN TIMES SQUARE.

And I have been seeing all this from someplace near Dick but now I am in my descending body and the crowd is rising up toward me and the bodies surge and hands clutch upward and I want to stop my transport beam I want to throw it in reverse and climb away from these hands and these upturned faces and these are not smiley faces these faces are full of shock and clutch and greed and grab and the hands, the thousands of hands that have surged together right beneath me, are ready to do the bidding of these faces which I realize is to pull what they believe to be useful bits off of my body as if I were some ancient saint whose bones are cracked into tiny pieces and enshrined in churches all over the world and these hands are ready to do this reverent work this holy dismemberment and I descend and I am almost reachable now and I wish to cry out some greeting but no words will come I have run out of words and then there are hands on me ten thousand heartless hands and I am plunged into darkness and there is only Dick Clark's voice saying, "Now that the spaceman has been torn to bits, it's time for our spotlight dance." But the music does not begin. There is silence, now, as well as the darkness. And then not even those things.

And my wife Edna Bradshaw is before me. "Honey, I've kept things warm for a few hours now because I didn't want to disturb you, you've been so tired and you were sleeping so sweetly. But I think it's time for supper and I was just fixing to set the table."

I sit up and I realize I have slept a long while. "What is the hour, by Earthtime?" I ask.

"It's getting on toward seven in the evening, Bovary Standard Time, as we used to call it," Edna says.

"I am glad you woke me," I say and I rise and I am struck by how far behind I am in my planning. I have not even decided where to appear, though I am prepared to take this most recent dream as

prophetic, as well. In spite of Times Square having a certain in-
trinsic logic as my point of descent, I realize that I have already
ruled it out. In the absence of more specific orders from my home
planet about how and where I am to show myself, I am ready to
allow my revelation to this world to begin more modestly.

"Thank you, my honeybun Edna Bradshaw," I say. "You go
on. I will wake our guests."

"I've set us up in the Reception Hall," she says and she scur-
ries out of the room, leaving a scent of sweet potato pie in her wake.

I have eaten my wife Edna Bradshaw's sweet potato pie before, prepared by her own hands for just the two of us on our
honeymoon, which we spent hovering over Niagara Falls. Edna had
always wanted to honeymoon at Niagara Falls. And with the smell
of sweet potatoes, this Earth thing is happening to me again, this
necessary engagement with all the stuff of the senses in the space
between one mind and another, and I find myself hovering there
once again and putting on my trench-coat-and-Chuck-Taylor disguise and scooting down to the planet's surface with my bride and
going with her to view the falls, which we did in the middle of the
night, the water rushing past and diving into the dark, both of us
excited, I think, at the risk of the moment, though at that time of
night I could have controlled the consciousness of anyone who
came near enough to find me actionably strange. We held each
other and leaned over the rail and the spray battered us and we
were, I realize, a tight little binary star system, the two of us, out
on the far edge of some wispy galaxy, and I think for a moment I
felt a sufficiency there, and I wonder if Edna Bradshaw felt the
same way, if she was freed from further yearning in the spray from
Niagara Falls.

But it is too late to ask. And I do not think the answer would
reflect its light upon the questions that now hurtle themselves

against me. And if there *were* a moment of complete contentment, it carried with itself the impossibility of its lasting, for in the next moment I surely looked back—my wife and I both surely looked back—and yearned for another moment as good as that one, and all things dissolved into change and striving.

And it is time for my last supper. And I must go and gather my guests. And I look back and I yearn for any moment but the moment that awaits me a few hours from now. And I go into the corridor and I glide along to these twelve where they mimic death and I will wave my hands and they will rise again and they will follow me.

I stop before them, twelve dreamers dreaming. And there are five places I have not yet entered, five visitors I will not have a chance to interview. I regret this, even as a familiar feeling comes over me, familiar and very strange at the same time. The five are clustered together at this near end of the sleeping corridor, three to my left, side by side, and two across from the three, also side by side. I look toward the first door to my left *and I fall from the sky toward a bull's-eye, the helicopter deck on a jack-up offshore drill rig, but there is no helicopter I am falling all on my own* and I look at the next door and *the flashbulbs are popping and I am crying already I am so happy and my glide on the Miss Texas runway is perfect with an invisible string attached to the top of my head and stretched taut all the way up to the sky holding me up straight and tall and beautiful like God's prettiest toy his wonderful Misty the marionette* and I look to the next door and I am feeling very uneasy suddenly *and I'm running as fast as I can through the thick trees through the vine-tangled trees and I dare to make a quick glance over my shoulder and I see the great scaled head of a dragon slung low in its pursuit and he's wearing a tuxedo and the coat sleeves are too short and his tie is crooked and he says, Okay let's take a chance let's fall in love* and I find I want to stop but I turn to

my right, to the first door and *I step toward the teacher's desk and
there is a vast shining light sitting there, an apple in front of him on the
desktop, and I know the light is God and I have no answers for his questions and I look around for Citrus, she's had some experience with this
dude, but she's nowhere in sight and I look at him, I look at God, and
he's this big glob of yellow light, like if phlegm was a Christmas decora-
tion, and I say, "The only way to love you is to hate religion," and he
smiles—don't ask me how* and I know I am inside their heads, even
now, as if they were of my own species, I have read Digger and
Misty and Mary and Jared but I am not happy about this, I find,
and yet I turn to the only one left, to Trey, to Trey the most devoted gambler from this bus of gamblers, and *I am before the slot
machine I've searched for all my life and it's big and it's bright with lights
and it smells of lavender and cookie dough and it's the Mama Slot and
there's no scale of winnings printed on it and there's no place for cash,
it's credit only, but that's okay I've got my Player's Preferred card and
it's attached to me, clipped to my pocket on a springy cord, like my mittens on the cuffs of my winter coat, and the card's coded with all the money
I have, every penny, and everything else I have, too, my clothes and my
furniture and my pots and pans and my potholders sewed by hand by
my mama and the card's got all my jokes, too, on its magnetic strip, and
all the tricks I know to try to beat the odds and it's got my memories,
every job every girl every drunken night, everything, and I slip the card
into the slot in the face of the machine and I pull the handle and the
windows whirl and whirl and whirl and I can see my mama there in the
whirling like this is one of those old peep-show machines and she smiles
at her little boy and the front door is open and the snow is swirling in all
around her and she's clipped my mittens to my sleeves and she says, Go
on now, Sweetie, and the light at the door is blinding white with the snow
and with the morning and I'm trying to figure my bet, which normally
should be easy, this game's a child's game and it's a thousand to one, ten*

thousand to one, that if I go out the door and down the street and into the school, she'll be here at the end of the day waiting for me, but this morning the snow is sparking in and I've got a gambler's hunch that it's time to stand pat, the odds are clear that you've got to draw the card but something's in your head saying not to do it, but I'm just a kid and I don't understand and she says, Go on now, you'll be late, and I'm feeling if I go out the door, she'll be gone when I get back home, but I don't trust my hunch and I go on out and one by one the windows in the Mama Slot stop whirling—click, she's at the kitchen sink—click, she's falling with her hands clutching her heart—click, she lies dead on the kitchen floor and she's alone and so am I, me and a lifetime left of hunches and I struggle to find my way back, it is time to find my way back to my own self, whatever that is now after all the years of voices and dreams, for I feel I am somehow changed. For one thing, I am ashamed at my powers, I am ashamed to be eavesdropping on these dark and private and vulnerable minds. So I stride up and down before the twelve doors and I wave my hands and I cry, "Come forth," and there is a stirring inside these places, inside the dark gape of these doorways, and I grow suddenly afraid, afraid even of these twelve, and then they appear, each doorway fills with a familiar self, and I say, "Hi, my name is Desi."

15

And the next thing I know, Edna has appeared beside me and she is making our guests feel right at home and telling them all about the Chicken Wiggle and her green salad with homemade Thousand Island dressing—no secret really, she confides, ketchup and mayo and sweet pickle relish—and they all seem entranced with these details and my wife Edna Bradshaw herds the twelve into a tight little gaggle—she is very skillful at this—and she moves them off down the corridor toward the Reception Hall. She looks over her shoulder at me and says, "You come on along whenever you feel ready."

She is a thoughtful wife. She is a prescient wife. Perhaps she knows more about what is inside me than I give her credit for. Perhaps they all do. Perhaps I know nothing about these creatures. I trail along. I am sad that I am outside the gaggle. But it is my fate.

We go in to the Reception Hall and the bus still sits in the middle but now, near the door, there is a great round table covered in a white cloth and set with thirteen places.

"Please," Edna says and motions to the table. "There are place cards."

And the twelve degaggle, pouring around both sides of the table looking at the cards. I step to the side of my wife Edna Bradshaw.

"There are only thirteen places," I say.

"Well I will certainly have my hands full serving all of you," she says. "I'll just catch a bite in the kitchen."

"I am sorry," I say.

"This is all you'll need to know about Earth. No need to go bothering everybody down there." Edna is making the statement that asks a question, for she is looking at me, waiting. She has asked, Are you still planning to go show yourself at midnight? I am afraid the answer I have for her is not the one she wants to hear. So I say nothing.

And there is a ruckus near the table.

"You can't be doing that," a voice says. I look up. It is Viola Stackhouse. Her arm is extended, her forefinger pointing across the table at Citrus, who stands by a chair with a place card in her hand. Arthur Stackhouse is already seated. Viola's other hand rests on his shoulder. She adds, "I know whose place that is. It's mine."

"Wouldn't you rather sit by your husband?" Citrus says.

"I'm happy to be next to our host," Viola says. " I *want* to be there."

"I know who he is," Citrus says.

"We all do," Viola says.

"Do you? Not like I know."

"He held my hands," Viola says. Then she bends to Arthur and clarifies, "Like a father."

"He's the father of everyone," Citrus says. "And he held my hands too. He held them and then he put me in my bed and he patted my hands. Patted them like a real father. Like the father most high."

"I could feel his heartbeat," Viola says.

I sense the snap of a head nearby. I look and Edna is thin-mouthed and brow-wrinkled, a look clearly intended for me.

"I could feel his heart too," Citrus says.

Edna's eyebrows plunge deeper and clinch toward one another.

"So could I, when he touched my hands." This is another voice.

Edna turns to look.

It is Claudia speaking. She goes on, "This is the spaceman's way with people."

"I am a friendly guy," I add.

And the faces turn toward me as if they are surprised to find me present in the room. They all seem more comfortable speaking about me than looking at me.

I take Edna's hand and I say to everyone, "This is my wife Edna Bradshaw. We are a happy couple. My species can give a heartbeat to anyone, but I have given my heart to Edna."

She looks up at me and her brow has loosened, she is smiling and her eyes, once more, are filling with tears. She lifts up—I presume on her tippy-toes—and she gives me a kiss on the cheek.

There are some sympathetic exhalations of air, wordless sounds that I value from this species, from the direction of the table: "Ah!" they say.

"Can I sit at your right hand, Father?" Citrus says.

"I've worked for NASA . . ." Claudia says.

"It was my place card . . ." Viola says.

"I can settle this easily," Hudson says. "He needs counsel at his right hand."

"You people are nuts, if you ask me," says Misty. "He's a spaceman."

"He is Jesus come again," Citrus cries.

Misty quickly amends her statement: "No offense intended, Mr. Desi. I just mean we should accept where you put us."

"You mean no harm. Am I right?" Digger says to me, drawing near Misty and slipping his arm around her.

"No harm at all," I cry. "Of course not. Please. Sit down. I want you to break bread with a friendly spaceman and I will pick your brains."

No fewer than half a dozen of my guests go wide-eyed and recoil at this. Fortunately I understand right away. "Please. I am using a phrase I have learned from you. My species does not literally 'pick at brains.' Heavens no. I merely seek your advice."

Viola leaves her husband and moves around toward Citrus. "Then who shall it be?"

"I think we need another place at the table," I say. "The one who serves us this meal shall sit at my right hand. My wife Edna Bradshaw."

Edna squeezes my hand. "Oh you spaceman. I guess I can manage. I'll get another chair."

"I'll help you," Viola says.

"Thank you, Sweetie," Edna says, and the two women move off.

I approach the table.

Citrus starts to move to the left of my chair, but Lucky is there and he flashes his place card at her.

Citrus's black lips tighten and she lowers her face.

"It is all right," I say to her. "You are near me wherever you sit."

She looks up at me. "Of course," she says. "Forgive the weakness of my faith."

I hesitate, trying to translate this observation. There is some body of knowledge standing between her and me now and I am sad for that, sad that I cannot speak to her and hear her directly. Before I can reply, she moves off to her place around the table.

Some of the guests are standing, some are sitting. "Please," I say, motioning to the chairs.

"This is all real strange, you know," says Trey.

Before I can answer, Citrus leaps in. "Don't you realize we're chosen people?"

"Chosen for what?" Digger asks, though he does not sound frightened.

"He loves us," Citrus says.

And I am struck motionless, where I stand, just behind my place at the table, my hand on the back of my chair. Then I have a reinforcement of this notion from a source close to me. Edna's voice from across the room, coming this way: "He's the most loving creature you'll ever find."

I look at her and she is carrying a tall, brushed-metal chair like all the others. She puts it beside mine and turns at once and heads off again. I set aside the question of love for the moment.

"You are all certainly *chosen*," I say. "Since these are the final hours of the observation phase, you are even more special."

"Is this the end of the world?" These words rise in a small and quavering voice from the far side of the table, from Mary Wynn, whose Vietnamese name means *generous*.

I cannot refrain from expressing my own fears at the moment. "Not of your world. No. Perhaps of mine."

Digger and Trey and Hudson remain standing. I say to them, "Please, gentlemen. I welcome you to my table. I am a friendly guy. My wife is the cook of your dreams. Please sit."

And they do. And I sit, as well. I am grateful to my wife. I am happy to be at this table with Chicken Wiggle and all the trimmings on the way. I am happy to be with these creatures. These people. These friends. These friends that I love. Yes.

I am looking around at their faces turned to me. And I wish to touch them, take their hands in mine. I wish to put this feeling I am having about them directly into the deepest recesses of their minds. And then I notice, sitting before me, a great glass pitcher of Presbyterian Punch. The liquid is very still in its pale greenness. There is a white froth on the top. I feel the coursing in my veins and I look at these faces as they wait and all their glasses are empty and I reach and take up the pitcher. I pour myself some punch first, just a little. I am afraid of this substance, but to give of myself I must overcome my fear. I must share this moment. I say, "This Presbyterian Punch is precisely the color of a spaceman's blood. Of my blood. Drink this and know that I love you all."

I pass the pitcher to Lucky who pours and passes it on and he holds his glass but he hesitates, he does not drink, and the pitcher moves to Claudia and she pours and the Presbyterian Punch flows into her glass and it feels as if it is coming directly from me, from my body, I feel an emptiness growing in me as the pitcher moves on and another glass is filled and another and I am growing weaker and my blood passes into the hands of one guest and another and another and they hold their glasses before them, waiting, though Misty starts to drink but Digger gently stops her with a touch on her arm and he nods to the other guests who are waiting and she waits too, and when Citrus pours from the pitcher she looks at me and she smiles in a knowing way and she says, "I knew you'd do this," and she passes the pitcher on and it moves and the voice of Edna Bradshaw is near me saying, "I am oh so sorry but I didn't realize till the last minute that I'm out of tea because of course this meal needs iced tea but it's all so festive, being New Year's Eve and the end of the millennium and all—though didn't we end one last year too?—anyway I thought something sweet to drink with dinner would be nice so I made Presbyterian Punch, which was such a big success when we all first met"—and I am glad Edna Bradshaw is here and Viola Stackhouse, too, for she is still beside my wife to help serve the dinner, and I say to them, though my voice is faint now from my weakness, "Please sit, both of you, drink with us," and they do sit and at last the pitcher is in the hand of my wife and there is enough left for a few fingers of punch in her glass and I am weak, I am empty, I feel in some literal way that I am in the hands of these twelve I snatched from the night as they chased their luck, these twelve I have chosen, and in the hands of Edna Bradshaw my wife, who I also chose, and she puts down the empty pitcher, and it takes a great effort even to raise this glass, but I do, and I say, "Please. Drink."

And Citrus says, "Do this in remembrance of Desi."

Some faces turn to her at this but then they all drink and so do I and I expect the taste of blood, the briny sea-taste of my spaceman's blood, but I am sweet I am bubbly I am the Pause That Refreshes and I feel myself filling up once more, as those around me drink, and I am restored. We all put our glasses down.

"That was nice," Edna Bradshaw says, and then she rises. "But if we're going to eat this dinner in the present millennium, I've got a few things to do." She goes off and as Viola starts to rise, Edna calls out, "It's okay, Viola honey. I can manage."

And they sit before me, waiting. In a few hours I must say crucial things to a planet full of strangers. These twelve sit before me now and I know them and they are getting used to me, and yet I have no words. I am in big trouble.

Abruptly, Trey breaks the silence. "I knew this was in the cards all along. I saw a UFO once. It had red and yellow lights on it and it moved real smooth over a tree line and then disappeared. It never left me, the sight of that."

"I saw one too," Digger says.

Misty shoots a glance across the table at her husband. "You never said."

"I am sorry to interrupt," I say. "But it is very unlikely that either of you saw us. Mr. Trey, where was this exactly?"

"Up in Michigan. About thirty years ago. I never forgot it."

"And you, Mr. Digger?"

"In a duck blind near the Gulf."

"That was swamp gas you both saw, the result of decaying vegetation releasing methane, hydrogen sulfide, and phosphine."

"Oh no," Trey says. "With all due respect, Mr. Spaceman, it was a certain winter day and I was stone cold sober and I saw what I saw."

"You bet." Digger punctuates his solidarity with Trey by slapping the palm of one hand down on the table. "I've seen swamp gas, and my UFO was entirely different."

I feel a bubble of irritation rising in my chest. "With all respect to you as well, Mr. Trey and Mr. Digger, but there is only one true source of UFOs on this planet called Earth. And that is from my home planet."

Trey makes one of the statements in the form of a question: "You saying there's nobody out there but you?"

"Of course not," I say. "But we are the only species to visit your planet."

"How do you know?" says Digger.

"Wait a minute," Citrus cries. "You all just aren't getting it, are you."

I am still engaged with Digger's challenge and I find my irritation growing. "Duh?" I say to him. "I am a spaceman. I should know."

"He's the one true spaceman," Citrus cries, "because there's only one true God."

"We always knew there was somebody bigger and better watching over us," says Jared. "One era, it's a carpenter. A whole other era, it's a spaceman."

"Hey," Citrus says to Jared. "Love grows."

"Love grows," Jared replies. I sense a semantic ritual between them.

Misty raises her hand as if she were seeking permission to talk in a schoolroom. But she speaks immediately, "Excuse me. Are we saying this spaceman is Jesus Christ or something?"

"Do you have nuclear weapons onboard this ship?" Arthur asks.

Viola flaps a hand across the table at her husband, "What are you talking crazy for?"

"It's not crazy," Arthur says. "I just want to know what our host has in mind for planet Earth."

"That's what we all want to know," Digger says.

"Hush," says Misty to Digger. "You can't always act like you're speaking for everybody."

Digger gives Misty a puzzled frown and a cock of the head. I sense that he is not accustomed to being criticized by her. Perhaps the circumstances have emboldened Misty.

"No one need be apprehensive about our intentions," I say. "As I explained when I first brought you onboard, I only wish to talk with you."

"My companion is a worrier," Hank says, softly. He is nearby, just beyond Edna and Viola. "We've been missing a couple of days, haven't we?"

"I am sorry for that. I realize there is a mystery surrounding you. We normally are very discreet about taking up our visitors."

Edna has appeared with a tray of salads, which she sets on a serving stand. Viola jumps up and Claudia begins to rise, too, though Viola waves her back down, saying, "Two's enough."

"Why have you suddenly become *indiscreet?*" I recognize Hudson's voice. I turn to him as a salad clunks down in front of me and I nod my head to him in respect.

I say, "This is a special circumstance. You will all be back on the planet in a matter of hours. And you will be my first visitors to retain their memory of all this."

My wife Edna Bradshaw sits down beside me, placing her own salad before her and declaring, "I just wanted him to have this final little meal with you all so he doesn't think he has to go down there tonight in person."

Hudson says, "You give us our memories, but if we tell the truth, we sound like lunatics."

"I will personally give you confirmation," I say. I pause and look at Edna, not wishing to dash her hopes in this public way, but I must explain myself to these people so that they might advise me.

Edna leaps into my pause. "This is the homemade Thousand Island dressing I was talking about on this salad here. I wanted to have shrimp cocktail, too, but this was short notice and I'm not able to shop on my own, as it were. There's special machines and all."

"This is fine," Viola says, lifting a forkful of lettuce dripping with the homemade dressing.

Another murmur goes around the table, affirming the quality of the salad. My wife Edna Bradshaw takes the compliments with a humble lowering of the face.

"What kind of confirmation?" Hudson asks.

I must think clearly now. And simply. It is time. I say, "At midnight I must descend in a public way and reveal to your planet the existence of my species and, by implication, the existence of a multitude of other species out among the stars."

Wordless sounds of surprise and interest come from the table at this announcement, but more noticeable for me is the severe cry of my wife's scooting chair. I look up at her, as she is now standing. She declares, "I must go and get the entree and so forth." But she goes nowhere. I look down from the struggle of her face to maintain its mask of the cheerful hostess and I see her hands trembling.

"Please," says Viola, "don't bother, Edna honey. You've done enough. We can all go out to the kitchen and serve ourselves."

"Of course," says Claudia. And then others say "of course" and "no problem" and they are all rising and Viola shows them the way to the kitchen.

Edna remains standing beside me, letting our guests serve themselves first. When we are alone I know I should speak to her but I am afraid. Then her hand is on my shoulder. "I'm sorry, Desi honey," she says. "I'm being a baby. A man is his work, I guess, and you have to do what you have to do because orders is orders no matter if it's dirty work because somebody's got to do it and if you can't be a help you should at least just get out of the way, which I want to do for you, out of respect, Desi, you honorable and obedient spaceman you, here's your sausage and there's the door." Her hand suddenly squeezes tight at my shoulder. "I'm going a little crazy here, I realize that, going crazy in my usual babbling way. But that's what you liked about me when you were first listening in to me and my friends with your machines before you and me ever met in the Wal-Mart Supercenter parking lot in Bovary. Isn't that so? Isn't that what you told me? That you liked the way I talked?"

I wish to affirm this to be true for my sweet and prolific wordmaker of a wife Edna Bradshaw, but she does not pause even for a breath with these questions, she rushes on, "And the proof was, after you heard me doing a lot of talking over a period of—what? months?—you asked me out for a date and then you asked me to marry you and that marriage proposal didn't happen because I'd clammed up, though part of me had been advising that, but I never did listen to that advice, you heard the real me and even so, you still wanted to marry me and that was a very sweet thing, a kind thing."

I insist now on the insertion of a few words of my own, regretfully overriding the voice of my wife. "It was not a kind thing, Edna Bradshaw," I say. "I *wanted* to marry you. I got what I wanted."

"See what a good idea this was?" she says, and she lets go of my shoulder and moves off toward her kitchen.

I do not follow her. I remain where I am. Now Jared is coming back with a plate full of food and Mary after him and Lucky right behind and others are following and I lower my face, turn my attention inward. I begin to hum soundlessly inside myself, an avoidance, I realize, a copping out, but I want now only to be left alone in my life—which, of course, would still include my wife Edna Bradshaw and our yellow cat Eddie—no, I *yearn* for the three of us to be left alone—I am afraid this is more than a simple *want*. And like so many *yearnings,* this is ultimately impossible to have, because for one reason, the yearnings inside all these individuals who are bearing their plates full of Chicken Wiggle to my table even now, *their* yearnings are an inseparable part of my most intimate concern, as well. I would carry a deep sense of all of them with me to my place of aloneness, and a deep sense, too, of all the others, all those I have interviewed over the years, those who have forgotten me utterly or who are dead. They, too, would follow me wherever I went.

I have one pleasant thought now. The memory of me, of Desi the Spaceman, will not pass from those who are sitting here at this table. And as the last of these coming from the kitchen—Viola Stackhouse—sits down, my hands flop foolishly about in front of me, striving to *do* something for them, for each of them, and there is a brush of warmth past my face and a wicker basket lands before me and a plate of food and Edna sits down with her own plate now and she motions to the wicker basket. "Why don't you pass the homemade buttermilk biscuits, Desi honey," she says.

And I take up the basket and I fold back the cloth and there are, within, many biscuits. I hold a great, steaming trove of Edna Bradshaw's homemade buttermilk biscuits, and I am happy to have these biscuits, for this is something I can do for these dear and fragile creatures before me—recognizing that I am myself fragile, that all sentient life in this universe is fragile—and I say, "Here, have some biscuits."

And I take one and I pass the basket to Lucky and he takes one and passes the basket on and the biscuits move around the table and I realize everyone is holding his or her biscuit, neither laying it down nor eating it, and the basket reaches Edna and she takes a biscuit and sets the basket before us. I gaze about the table. "Why are you all not eating?" I ask.

Some of my guests look down at their biscuits and they, too, seem puzzled, but still no one is eating. And then Citrus says, "They're beginning to understand, is why. We're waiting for you to break the bread."

And I look at the biscuit in my hand. And I look up at all the faces turned to me.

And I say, "Nothin' Says Lovin' Like Somethin' from the Oven."

Then I break the biscuit, and one voice—I do not exactly know which one, because it remains isolated for only the briefest of moments—a voice begins, "Nothin' . . ." and the rest of the voices—

all of them, I think—instantly join in, and all the voices say, "Nothin' Says Lovin' Like Somethin' from the Oven."

And I have broken my biscuit in two and they all break their biscuits in two and all eyes are on me and I do not like to have anyone watch me eat, especially not members of another intelligent species, but everyone is clearly waiting for me and I put one piece of the biscuit in my mouth. It is, by the code of daily conduct adhered to in Bovary, Alabama, far too big a piece of biscuit, but my mouth is large and the pressure on me is great and so I take in half a biscuit and I wait until the others turn away before I chew, since I expect to inadvertently expel crumbs of my biscuit in the process. But they have all done what I did. They have all taken fully half a biscuit into their mouths and their cheeks are pooched out and they are still watching me, still not chewing.

So I chew. And they chew.

"See how nice this all is?" Edna Bradshaw says, though her words are muffled through the biscuit. I discern an ongoing nervousness in my wife, since, by the same Bovarian standards, she normally would not be speaking with her mouth full.

"Nice," Viola says, sending some crumbs forth onto the table.

"Very nice," Misty says, also spewing crumbs. "Excuse me," she appends, with the same result for which she seeks absolution, and she claps her hand over her mouth.

"It is all right," I say, spewing crumbs myself, wishing no one to feel ill at ease.

"Thank you." Misty releases more crumbs.

"Yes," says Claudia, "it's all very nice." Still more crumbs.

"Hallelujah!" cries Citrus, her face slightly lifted, her biscuit crumbs arching high. And others express their pleasure at the biscuits and the dinner and at things in general, I believe, saying "these are good" and "this really is nice" and "let's eat" and the air over the table is filled with white bits of Oven-Fresh Homemade Goodness, the spirit of this dinner made tangible before us.

And I look down at the plate of food before me. The main dish is a complex thing, bits of green peas and red pimento and tan mushrooms all awash in the swirls of egg noodles and, of course, there are white chunks all through, and I am stricken again with the fear that I cannot shake. These chickens died for us: I put it this way to cast it in its least frightening light, though the chickens were slaughtered and diced nonetheless. They died to nourish these other creatures, to give them life. It is the pattern repeated over and over on this planet, these very chickens, for instance, being willing to eat insects scurrying about. And, I must admit, it is a pattern found throughout the universe, though my own species has ceased the practice. We eat no sentient thing. Still, one wonders about even the possible hidden sentience of vegetables. There is so much yet that my species does not know. All of which thinking represents the wild spiral of a mind away from a fear for his own skin.

"Am I this chicken?" I ask.

For a moment the others do not understand what I mean. Then Hudson says, "I'd sure be, facing what you're facing."

Now I am puzzled. But I know to set aside my literalist impulse at moments like these. I suddenly remember the idiom. To be a *chicken* means to be afraid. This makes things much worse. Those whom I will face tonight understand the chicken to have feelings. Particularly the feeling of fear. And so how must they understand, then, the way in which they make billions of these fellow creatures end their lives? Prematurely. Ravished with fear. Grabbed and beheaded. Plucked and gutted and cooked and eaten. It is imbedded in the very *words* of this place that chickens are fearful creatures, yearning, no doubt, for a life free from that fear. How can I face those who willfully scorn such feelings in others?

I look at these twelve around the table, their teeth grinding away at the flesh of others. These thirteen. For my wife is eating, as well. It was her choice to serve chicken. And yet I know how gentle and loving is my Edna Bradshaw.

"What all is it you've got to do, exactly?" asks Hudson. "Tonight down on Earth."

I find myself saying by rote, "At midnight I must descend in a public way and reveal to your planet the existence of . . .

Hudson interrupts, "Right. Right. But then what?"

"This is what I am still trying to determine," I say.

Digger says, "Pretty late in the day, isn't it?"

"Yes," I say, "I am afraid it is."

Claudia leans in my direction, her hand coming out. "Don't you have specific directions for what to say, what to do after the revelation? That sort of thing?"

"No," I say. And another clear but wordless reaction occurs. A dark, sinking thrum of a sound from those at the table. I am in trouble, they clearly believe.

"We are like this, as a species," I say. "I am the senior specialist on this planet. So those to whom I am responsible give me my directive in the simplest way and allow me to carry it out however I see fit."

Hudson says, "But how about envoys and technical advice and such."

"All of that is premature," I say. "You must come to grips with the fundamental principle before any of those secondary things can happen."

"So that's it?" Hudson asks.

"It?"

"You go down, say here I am, and you split?"

I struggle with literalism once more. Hudson notices. "Leave," he says. "You leave."

"Yes."

"Right away?" He is saying he does not approve.

"Right away is up to me," I say. And then, "This is good." I am suddenly full of gratitude to Hudson, and to the others as well, for pressing me. "This is good you should ask these questions. I need your help to understand how to proceed."

There is a general squaring of shoulders and clearing of throats. I believe my guests are pleased at being cast in this role.

"Don't they . . . *you* . . . want any further contact with us after you show yourself?" Claudia asks, an edge to her voice.

"Not for a time," I say. "We hope this basic fact of things will encourage you to end your divisiveness. You are one people, all of you. We will stay away until you learn to live with each other."

The edge smooths in Claudia's voice. "You've done this else-where?"

"Not me personally. But as a species, yes."

Lucky, next to me, bends a little in my direction. "How does it usually go?"

"It is not fair to compare," I say.

"So you don't expect the planet Earth to change very quick," Hudson says.

"Do you?" I hear how naturally now my own instinctive choice of *words* employs the strange question-as-statement locution. This pleases me.

And Hudson nods at me with a smile that I find pleases me, too—more, it makes me very happy—a we-understand-each-other smile. And Lucky's leaning toward me makes me happy. And the earnest attentiveness of all these faces makes me happy. "My friends . . ." I say, though I have nothing in mind to finish the sentence. It is a simple assertion of being. They wait. "That is all," I say. "You are my friends."

Digger puts both hands on the table, "So what is it you need our help deciding?"

"Who you all are, the people of Earth." I am not surprised to find blinking and bewildered sighing at this. As soon as I speak, I recognize the original goal of this dinner has never been realistic. So I quickly let them off the hook. "But I do not expect that from you. You have given me enough by your patience on this ship."

"Then, what?" Digger asks.

"What to say down there." Again, all that I do is speak the need and I instantly know I cannot be helped. I say, "But the words must come from me. I realize that. It would be a mistake to take your suggestions, no matter how good, and parrot them."

"So is there nothing?" Viola sounds disappointed.

Citrus rises to her feet. "There's one thing. A big thing that only we can do for Desi. We will speak what we know of this Second Coming, after he is . . ." She gropes for a word. She settles on ". . . gone."

"You are right, Citrus," I say. "I must descend in a place where very many people will see me, including the Cable News Network. But your memories of me and this ship and my wife Edna Bradshaw and her Homemade Southern Goodness will be very helpful to focus people's understanding."

"Oh man!" Hudson cries. "A book deal."

"The Larry King Show," Claudia says.

"I'm frightened," says Mary.

Lucky shifts beside me, his hand going out toward his girlfriend around the curve of the table. "It's okay," he says.

"Yes," I say to her, "there is no responsibility . . ."

"It's hard enough trying to be what I am," she says.

"Nobody ever heard of Thaddeus or James the son of Alphaeus." This is from Citrus, who is still standing. We all look at her, and she adds, "They were part of the first twelve. You don't have to be a major player."

"Are we still trying to say that Mr. Desi is Jesus?" Misty asks.

"I am not Jesus," I say. Firmly.

"You are *next*," Citrus says.

"I am . . ."

"It's all made new," Citrus says. "It's always got to be made new."

"I am Desi."

"My daddy will never recognize you," Citrus says.

"Actually I am not originally *Desi* . . ."

Citrus lifts both her hands high, her palms turned upward. "There will be many who will not recognize you."

"My wife Edna Bradshaw has given me that name."

"They will turn on you."

"You cannot pronounce my original name."

"They will crucify you."

With that, declared loudly by Citrus, everything stops. I, of course, am drawn instantly back from my tangent about my name. The local murmuring—I presume about the opportunities for appearances on late-night talk shows and endorsements of various products—suddenly ceases. We all look at Citrus. She is looking at me. Her hands are still raised, but in the silence she slowly lowers them.

Then Hudson says, "Where exactly do you plan to appear?"

"Yes," I say. "This is something that you *can* help me with."

"New York City," Citrus says at once. "Times Square."

I am growing frightened again. Of Citrus sounding like a prophet. Citrus giving voice to the worst that might happen to me. Citrus, now, tapping into *my* dream. Times Square.

And Hudson frightens me, too. "That's the logical choice," he says.

I know it is logical.

"Big media," says Digger.

"I'm worried," says Claudia.

"It's the *only* choice," says Citrus.

"Worried about what?" My wife Edna Bradshaw breaks her silence at all of this. She is speaking to Claudia.

Claudia turns to Edna and motions toward Citrus. "What she said. If there's a danger of a crucifixion for an unarmed spaceman suddenly appearing in a flying saucer and scaring the hell out of a big, drunken crowd, that's the place for it."

"If?" I ask.

"There *is* a danger," Claudia says.

"There is an *inevitability*," says Hudson.

"Houston would be no better." I turn to the voice. It is Hank. He makes fists with his two hands, extends his two forefingers and thumbs, and then snaps his thumbs down and up. I do not understand.

Hudson explains it to me. "Guns. They carry them in their cars."

Lucky, at my side, leans to me again. "*Any* big crowd is going to freak out."

"I'm afraid that's true," says Claudia.

"Does it have to be tonight?" Edna's voice is tiny in my ear.

I turn to her. I know how hard it is for her to hear all of this. "I am sorry, my honeybun. This is one of the few things my orders specifically require. Your planet sees this as an auspicious moment."

I feel a sharp pain at this phrase coming from my mouth: "*your* planet." I am apart. I am separate, in some important sense even from my wife Edna Bradshaw.

"Come with us to the casino." Edna looks in the direction of this voice. I do, too. It is Trey.

"That's a good idea," Edna says, brightening. "We can all go together."

There are strong temptations before me now. I am afraid this dinner has been a mistake. I am who I am. I say, "It is necessary to have a big crowd. It is necessary to have major media. Videotape. Slow motion. Freeze frame. Playing over and over for years to come. Regrettably, this discussion must come to a close now."

I am afraid they hear a sharpness in my voice that I do not intend. They all fall silent and grim.

Then Edna says, "I think it's time for pie."

"Please serve our guests," I say. I am Bluer Than Blue. "I will have no pie. My time approaches. I must be alone now and prepare myself."

I rise.

Trey says, "I thought you were going to tell us how to win big at the casino."

"That was just me shooting off my mouth like I always do," says Edna. "I'm sorry if I misled you. I just wanted you to understand what a smart and good man my husband is." I do not have to look at her to know that the tears are beginning to well up in her eyes.

I am feeling guilty at not fulfilling the promise made in my name. I think about what I have learned on this subject. I say, "Play the handle. There are four clicks. Jump into the moment. Know how much you're willing to lose, and when you lose it, get up and find your way to the door."

There is a moment of silence. Then Trey says, "That's it?"

"I am not as smart as I look," I say.

"And you're talking to a guy they nicknamed 'Trey.' Not 'Ace.' I need a little more."

I stand here wishing I can be more helpful and finding nothing to say, and then Hudson speaks up, catching Trey's attention and addressing him. "If Desi does what he says and lets us remember all this and take our story with us, he's giving you something a lot more valuable than some gambling tips. Book deals. Lecture tours. Oprah's show. You're a made man . . . Ace."

"You will all remember," I say. "I want you very much to remember." And saying this, I turn and Edna touches my hand. I manage to smile at her and I know she understands that I must be alone.

I go out as Edna cries "Who wants pie?" and a chorus of voices says "I do!" and I am glad they will get what they want.

16

I move away from the sounds of the others, into the quiet of the corridors of my ship. I am blank inside. Inside my head, that is. Somewhere else inside me—in the very somewhere else I have been learning about from the people on this planet—I am filled too full. I want, I yearn, I yak yak yak, I yada yada yada, I make a turn and another and I go in at a door without thinking and I am in the Hall of Objects. I stop. There is a hush in the air. There is a dim blue light all around. The shelves are full of bits of the planet Earth. I wait for just the right moment. One click. Two. Three. I listen. To the soundless welter. Inside and out. I move forward. And I am. A garden troll and a Swiss Army knife and an adding machine large as the portable TV on one side of it and as silver as the Pontiac hubcap on the other side and there are more hubcaps and more and more stored in stasis elsewhere and a multitude of umbrellas and single gloves and socks—we have collected many socks, but only one from each set—and The Club to protect your car, to keep the bad guys from getting what they want, and a Heated Massaging Body Mat with Magnets with a woman on the box lying on her side and her head is thrown back and she is feelin' groovy like the Feelin' Groovy Barbie doll beside her with spaghetti-strap fuchsia minidress and knee-length iridescent coat with faux fur at the cuffs and hem and hot pink drop earrings all setting off her lovely black hair and lavender eyes and a wingless Quacker the Beanie Baby Duck with original tag, old-style, and a lava lamp birthing an orange sun, even now, and I am floating on the crest of these waves inside me, they crash beneath me, but as they do, others come along and bear me up, me, and I am a Krazy Kat Klock ticking away the last ticks of my time before me, the eyes darting back and forth, and Mr. and Mrs. Potato Head standing side by side waiting for me to speak, to tell them what my existence means to them, waiting to ask me to interchange their facial features to make new delightful combinations of them both, and I am a bag of golf clubs and a Weed Eater and a painted saw with a great green stretch of countryside and a barn and cows and an orange sun and I am a Soap-on-a-Rope and a three-bladed razor with rubber fins and a bowling-pin cocktail shaker and a Tom Corbett Space Cadet steel lunch box and a St. Joseph Home Sale Kit with plastic Saint Joseph to bury in the yard of your handyman's fixer-upper to make it the house of someone's dreams, someone with good credit, and I am reeling now, I am feeling snagged as if by this Popeil's Pocket Fisherman before me, I am being dragged from my watery world into this other world of air and light and a glow-in-the-dark rosary taller than me and a Crosley tabletop cathedral radio and I am The Body Hug the full-length pillow to hold in the night and it conforms to your very own body contours and it is easy to care for and it is odorless, and this is the hook in me, the loneliness of these things, the terrible striving in these things, and I am a battery-operated mustache trimmer and a nose-hair clipper and pre-trimmed prefeathered self-adhesive long and lovely eyelashes and a Water Bra more natural than any other padded bra (not for prolonged use in cold weather) and a wolf-whistling furry monkey who says I love you—and what am I to do about all of this what am I to do and where am I to go?—and I am a brass Statue of Liberty, her lamp lifted and her belly a thermometer, and I am, beside her, a cast-iron Empire State Building, also with thermometer, and I stop here before them, and there is a necessary thing for me to do and there is a logical place for me to go—Little Old New York New York the Big Apple the Big Burg the Big City Father Knickerbocker the Empire City Jumpin' Jitterburg the Melting Pot the Little Old Hell of a Town If I Can Make It There I Can Make It Anywhere— and I see out of the corner of my eye the blue-black metallic gleam of Claudia's pistol, but I do not look at this object, I focus to see what the temperature is, and it is both seventy-two and eighty-one, and for a moment there is no logic at all, there is only the jostle of *things* and a clock somewhere—perhaps Krazy Kat, perhaps an- other—clanging an alarm—and I am a poor and huddled mass yearning to breathe free, but I am not free, it is nearly time and I am bound to go. I am homeless and tempest-tossed, and I have my own lamp to lift.

17

And so I find myself standing beside the door of the bus that bears its *LUCK* upon its face and my time has run out and my *LUCK* has, too, I am afraid, and my wife Edna Bradshaw is at my side and the twelve who will remember me—these dear twelve—are ready to return. I shake each hand that passes before me, wishing to give at least a beat or two of my heart. But it is difficult. My hands are stiff. My fingertips are puckered. And I am missing important things, I realize. I have fallen out of *the moment,* in violation of one thing I think I can say I have learned from this planet, but there is nothing to do about it because even the process of thinking about what I am missing makes me miss even more of those things, and I have only fragments: Digger's mouth sets hard, Misty's eyes fill with tears, I am speaking words to them and they are passing on into the warm good-bye of my wife Edna Bradshaw and I do not catch what they are saying, I am forgetting their faces already as they may forget me, too, even without my help, and ". . . luck . . ." comes in Trey's voice and he is passing on and I am wishing luck to him in return, I think, but I can hear my own heart now, thumping in my head, I am aflame with fear and Mary's hand is moist and her eyes are moist and she is gone and Lucky says something about eagles and his eyes also are filling and I am working myself up even more and Arthur is here and gone and now Viola's face looms into mine and she speaks of knowing when to fold your hand and there are more of these tears, these baffling tears, Viola's eyes are full, and now they are overflowing, and things suddenly slow down. My hearing clarifies. Viola has moved on and my wife is saying, "Viola, honey, I wish I could give you a phone number or something."

"Me too," Viola says. "You beam me up anytime you want some help shopping."

The two women laugh and Jared is shaking my hand. I turn to him. "This is all so out-there," he says.

"Thank you," I say.

He moves along to the warm murmuring of my wife and I expect to find Citrus next but it is Hank grasping my forearm with his free hand as we shake. "Drive safely," I say. "But not until your wheels touch the highway."

"You be safe, too," he says, and he steps to Edna.

Claudia, Hudson, and Citrus are the only ones remaining outside the bus and they are all hanging back, shifting their feet and trying, I think, to be the last one to say good-bye.

"There is no time to hesitate," I say to them, and Claudia shoots the other two a little disgusted glance and comes forward.

"Good-bye, Desi," she says. "Thanks for answering at least one of the big questions."

"You are not alone," I say.

Claudia smiles. "Neither are you," she says.

"Wait," I cry, suddenly remembering the glint of metal in the Hall of Objects. "I still have your pistol."

"Keep it," she says. "That's one small step for woman."

Claudia lowers her face abruptly, I believe to hide the tears, and she moves on.

I turn and I find Hudson turning, too, and we are both failing to see Citrus. Hudson shakes his head. "She's trouble, man."

"I am sure she will show up when you get on the bus."

Hudson nods and extends his hand and I shake it. "Look," he says. "Your orders don't require you to *maximize* the risk, do they?"

"No," I say. "I do not read them that way."

"Then don't. Find yourself a nice quiet place."

"But it cannot be quiet. This impression I make will have to last."

Hudson shrugs and he softly claps me on the shoulder. "Then try to take care of your skinny ass, you hear?"

"Meeting you was money from home," I say.

Hudson is briefly confused by this but then he smiles.

He steps away, toward my wife Edna Bradshaw, and she says to him, "You sure you don't want me to wrap up a piece of the sweet potato pie for you?"

And as Hudson begins politely to decline this offer, Citrus's voice whispers close to my ear, "I will not deny you thrice. Not even once."

"Good," I say and she is very near, turned the same way I am, as if she is hiding behind me.

"Remember," Citrus says, "He did not climb down from the cross. He saved others, Himself he could not save."

"I am a friendly guy," I say.

"New York," she says.

"A regular Joe," I say.

"Times Square. It's your Calvary."

"What is this?" my wife Edna Bradshaw says. "You cute little thing, still wearing that stuff on your lips makes them look like they're about to fall off from the barn rot, you come on over here and say good-bye to your friend Edna and make a promise to let me do you a makeover someday."

Edna has dragged Citrus by the hand toward her, but Citrus jerks free and lurches back toward me.

"Please," she says. And she stands before me, not sure herself what she is to do. "Father," she whispers. Then, "Master." She closes her eyes and a dark thing comes over her and she opens her eyes and she slides up against me and she kisses me on the cheek.

I see my destiny. Millions of eyes are upon me. I descend and the eyes grow wide and the bodies surge and the hands clutch.

"You go on, get aboard now," Edna is saying.

The press and heat of Citrus is gone from me now.

I look and she is going up into the bus and Hank is standing there in the doorway, turning aside to let Citrus pass, but he is looking at me.

Then there is only Hank in the doorway and he squares around. "Mr. Desi," he says.

The crowd is still in my head. A million voices—two million—rise in fear and then in rage and I am aflame, A Flame with Such a Burning Desire. For what? For what?

Hank says, "You should appear in New Orleans. They might understand there."

"The Big Easy," I say.

"It's just down the highway."

"Let the Good Times Roll," I say.

"I'm sure they've got a big party tonight," he says. "Plenty of media."

"Thank you for the suggestion."

"*I'd* be comfortable there," Hanks says, and he winks and he nods and he disappears into the dimness of the bus and the door closes.

Then a hand and arm of my wife Edna Bradshaw comes in through my arm and she is beside me and holding on tight and we cross the great floor of the Reception Hall together. We turn at the door and a panel is there, which I open, and faces are pressed against the windows all along this side of the bus. Our friends are looking at us and waving and Edna and I wave in return. Then I touch the panel and the Reception Hall is filled with a bright light and the floor beneath the bus slides open and the bus descends, the hands still waving, the bus sinks down till the faces dip beneath the level of the floor and then the waving fingertips are gone and the roof of the bus and the floor slides and it seals itself shut and the light vanishes and there is a sudden jagged clutch of fear inside me, as if my friends have just gone down with a great ship to a watery grave. But I know their wheels will soon be spinning on Interstate 10. They will be chasing their luck once more. And so will I.

18

When a girl from Bovary, Alabama, finds herself married to a bona fide spaceman and she goes away to far galaxies and tries to be a good wife out there in outer space, in spite of all her life up to then she being afraid of change and taking a chance and going too far from home—and let's face it, when I say "girl" I don't mean "girl," I mean a forty-something woman who prior to this extraordinary thing happening to her had a life of what they call, in the hairdressing parlors of Bovary, "dignified simplicity" or sometimes "simple Southern grace" or sometimes just "lost hopes and blown chances"—I can admit all that now, being forty-plus and having a life like that—so when such a woman like me finds herself alone in an invisible spacecraft sitting in a field of witch grass out behind the place where her motor home once sat, the very place where her spaceman husband parked this very craft on the night he came a-courting her after having met her in the parking lot of the all-night Wal-Mart Supercenter, like God Himself had wanted us to meet—when she finds herself sitting there and she's all alone in an alien vessel except for her yellow cat Eddie purring on her lap and she doesn't know whether her dear sweet spaceman husband is being ripped to pieces by an angry Earth mob even at that very moment, and she being under directions from him to wait for two hours after midnight, New York City Time, and if she doesn't get his radio message by that time she is to push a certain button and step out of this machine and try to resume her life in her former hometown and try not to read the newspapers for a few days because under those circumstances the news was certainly going to be bad about what had hap-

pened to her husband, and when a woman like that—who's me, of course—even has a way to make a record of her voice while she waits, which her husband has showed her as he is saying good-bye and putting her in this spacecraft and is giving her a kiss in that sweet lipless way of his—though being lipless isn't a way, exactly, it's more like a condition, which just goes to show how much I love him because the touch of his spaceman mouth is about as happy a thing for me as I could ever imagine and I pray that I will have a chance to be that happy again—but he gave me a kiss and he showed me what to do and here I sit, and in a situation like this, even with the chance to talk—and I don't think there's a tape or anything in this thing to run out, I can go on as long as I want—but when a woman—even a woman like me—finds herself in a situation like this, she is pretty much left at a loss for words, which is what I am right now. Except to say that when the door was closing and I was looking at my spaceman husband maybe for the last time ever, he began to do something I have never seen him do.

Desi wept.

19

Citrus's kiss is still burning on my cheek when my hand goes to the ship's guidance panel. My wife Edna Bradshaw, along with our yellow cat Eddie, has already been dispatched to wait in a place where she can resume a life on Earth if her spaceman husband in fact fulfills the destiny of Murdered God.

And I wept. In sending Edna Bradshaw away not knowing if I would ever see her again, I at last found my way to the Earthlings' private sea. I opened a door inside me and there it was, and I strode forward and into the waves and there were voices all around me, all the voices I had taken into my own mouth, all the voices who knew how to live intensely in that sensual space out there between one mind and another, and the sea rose up and filled my eyes and I closed the door of the shuttle craft and Edna was weeping too.

And yet, poised now before the guidance panel, it is not the track of my first tears that I am feeling as I make these last decisions that will seal my fate, it is Citrus's kiss, a kiss that burns like a brand on my body. And the brand is NYC. New York City. I am Signed Sealed 'n' Delivered. I even move my hand and my spaceship slides smoothly across Louisiana and Mississippi and Alabama and so forth, picking up the Appalachian Mountains in Virginia and all I can think is, New York Here I Come. And yes, I understand that this coming I am about to make—the coming of a real-live rootin'-tootin' no-doubt-about-it space alien—especially at this millennially portentous moment—will be just about as big, news-wise, on planet Earth as if I were the coming of the man Citrus believes me to be.

But even as I think those things, I also think of my chosen twelve racing through the night. Come to Louisiana For to Have Some Fun. Then I think of Hudson's words, and Hank's. I do not have to maximize the risks. There might be a place more inclined to accept me. And I think of my great yummy pecan ball of a wife sitting in the place where I came to woo her, frightened for me now, expecting to be widowed. And I think about me. Me me me me me. Why not me? I am. That is me. What does me want? What does me *yearn* for?

Okay, I think. Okay. I move my hand and I am back in Louisiana. I speed to the Crescent City, the Queen of the South, the City that Care Forgot, New Orleans. And I consult the information we have on the place and midnight is approaching and I hover now twenty miles directly above the exact spot in New Orleans that seems to me, from what is known by our research, to be the exact right spot for my purpose, and I magnify the image of New Orleans on my screen and I see the curve of the Mississippi River through the French Quarter and there is a public park and a square and I zoom in on this image and I see my destination and I magnify it and this choice of New Orleans was no cop-out, I realize. There is a vast throng of people here, too, also prone to freak out, I presume, and Hank was right, there is plenty of media. Too much of all of that, people and media and the potential for mass terror. I can feel no difference between this and Times Square. And I am seizing up just as badly here. But I cannot compromise any further.

And so, I put my spacecraft on a timed instruction. I place a transmitter to the ship's voice recorder on the lapel of my freshly starched white shirt with my Tabasco necktie and gray pin-striped suit, and I am ready, if I die, to send this vessel, empty of all but voices, back to my home planet on its own. My epitaph. And I will be content, at least, that my wife will have her old life back. Content to have the bits and pieces of my body dispersed by fire or worms or the deep sea or even held in stasis in jars in secret government labs. Content with that. Yes. Content because I will, in death, be here, on the planet Earth. Content because I will thus, in a sense, remain close to Edna Bradshaw and close to Minnie Butterworth and close to Whiplash Willie Jones and to Herbert Jenkins and to Viola Stackhouse and Hudson Smith and Claudia Lambert and all the rest of them. And that is the Bible.

And I move my hand and my spaceship descends, straight down, from twenty miles above Jackson Square in the French Quarter of New Orleans, Louisiana, to ten miles above to five to one and the ship is cloaked and invisible, and on the screen I see the crowd roiling in anticipation, for the millennium has only a little more than a minute left in it and I am coming, I am coming to you, planet Earth, you will soon understand, and I am half a mile above and a quarter mile and my hand now is poised to uncloak this craft and my body is roiling like the crowd, roiling with the heat of the stars that you creatures there below know only as tiny bits of ancient light, I fall to you, I fall and I move my hand now and I make the ship visible to everyone and beneath me is St. Louis Cathedral with three spires, the center one, the tallest, pointing straight up at this wondrous sight, this vessel from outer space. I place the craft on its automatic settings and quickly I glide to the center of the control room.

And I wait, stiffly, Without a Song in my Heart, and the light flares, fills my eyes, catches me tight, and I begin to sink down. I close my eyes and I try to Whistle a Happy Tune, but my mouth is too rigid to pucker and I am free of the ship and I am in the night

air and I open my eyes, there are corridors of light and blooms of
fireworks and a steady roar of human voices beneath me and I look
down and the high center spire is aimed right at me and I move
my hand and adjust the beam and I slide out, and the square before the cathedral unfolds before me, teeming with life, and I am
ready to see them, see all these faces turned up to me, to this extraordinary sight, a spaceman in a felt hat and gray suit with hot-
sauce bottles floating on his tie coming down in a beam of light. I
focus. I blink my big old spaceman eyes and I concentrate my
superior vision and I am descending into a great sea of plumes and
feathers and masks and I look harder as I descend and I am passing the highest tip of the spire and I descend toward an enormous
pink rabbit—the Energizer battery bunny who Keeps On Going—
and a human Coke can, a face framed in the ring of the pull tab,
and a woman warrior with plastic breastplates and brandishing an
aluminum-foil sword and a nearly naked King Neptune with tri-
dent and sea-shell jockstrap and a man shrouded in a great, full-
body rubber sheath with French Tickler top and a gang of bikers
in black leather but with great swaths of their jackets and pants
missing showing their flesh beneath, and I look more widely at the
crowd and some faces are clearly focused on me, some hands point
and wave, and I realize I am missing my opportunity, I am being
the spectator not the show, and I wave in return and a trio of nuns,
side by side, see me and they return my wave and then in unison
they clap their hands against the center of their chests—it is the
mea culpa, they feel they have sinned—and I am about to spread
my hands before them, to offer them reassurance, but before I do,
they all three open wide the fronts of their habits and expose their
breasts—three pairs of pink, wondering eyes stare up at me—and
the habits close and the nuns acknowledge the applause of those
around them and they receive the kisses of the bikers and I am

falling into confusion in this column of light and I scan the crowd, trying to understand, and suddenly I realize that I have won, at last, the attention of much of the crowd, I feel all eyes on me, and the nuns have taught me something—a precious lesson I should have learned already—I have dressed in my suit and shirt and tie, as if I were an Earthling myself—what a basic blunder I have made—and I rip off my hat and my tie, and my spaceman face, at least, is nakedly clear—I will not fail in what I must do—I heighten my voice to be heard far and wide and I do not plan what to say, I trust the words to come, and I begin, "I am a friendly guy come from a distant planet. You are not alone." And though my voice is loud, the crowd is louder—they are not alone, they are one voice, uttering a sound like the sea, roaring in a storm—and I am descending farther, getting closer and closer, but I sense the moment of all eyes being on me has passed, most of the eyes have remained where they were even as I have moved—in spite of my face being clearly visible now—and I glance back and above me and it is the clock they were watching—and they still are—the new millennium is coming, only seconds away, and they are focused on this moment, on this moment in their senses, in the company of each other, and I look out at them and they are indeed a vast sea, they are moved by a great rising wave, all of them together, bunny and biker, Neptune and nun, Coke can and condom, they are one people, and I know why I have made my blunder, why I descended dressed as one of them, and I fall in my column of light past the great front doors of the cathedral and I know my own yearning clearly now, even as a man in ostrich feathers and a woman in combat fatigues press back against the crowd to make a place for me. And the crowd cries out "Three, two, one!" and then there is a great roar and my eyes are full of tears and the wave lifts us all and I swim into the crowd hugging and being hugged, kissing and being kissed.

20 I am. Still. I am more than ever. I sent the ship back to where it came from. I told my species to stay away for a century or two, at the very least. My wife Edna Bradshaw and I have taken a little place in an old slave house in a courtyard full of jasmine and bougainvillea in the French Quarter of New Orleans. Edna does hairdressing. People talk to her. She talks to them. She is happy about that, though I will be forever grateful to her for her willingness to give up those things to be my wife, when we could never have expected this outcome. Eddie the yellow cat likes our little place, too, though I sometimes must rescue a gecko from his grasp.

I feel at home here. I work in Jackson Square. My colleagues are the fire-eaters and the jugglers and the painters and the fortune-tellers. I sit at a little table and my sign says, TALK WITH A SPACE-MAN. I do what I have always done. I listen to the voices of this planet, one at a time. I am a good listener. Some people think I really am a spaceman, an incarnate glimpse into the infinite and mysterious elaboration of the universe. Some people think I am just one of them in costume, an Earthbound creature caught in time and yearning his way along. Look around. Listen to each other. I am both, and so are you. So let's go around the corner, you and I, and get a flaming dessert together. Lately I've been thinking there's a revelation to be had from a sweetly burning banana.